陇东红色歌谣选译

（汉英对照）

Translation of Selected Longdong Red Songs

(Chinese-English Edition)

闫晓茹／译

审定　李旭

顾问　闫果知　〔美〕Keenan Madson

四川大学出版社

2018年庆阳市重点文艺创作项目资助出版

陇东学院学术著作基金资助出版

项目策划：余　芳
责任编辑：余　芳
责任校对：周　洁
封面设计：墨创文化
责任印制：王　炜

图书在版编目（CIP）数据

陇东红色歌谣选译 ： 汉英对照 / 闫晓茹译． — 成都 ： 四川大学出版社， 2019.11
ISBN 978-7-5690-3165-2

Ⅰ．①陇… Ⅱ．①闫… Ⅲ．①民歌－作品集－甘肃－汉、英 Ⅳ．①I277.242

中国版本图书馆 CIP 数据核字（2019）第 248791 号

书名　陇东红色歌谣选译（汉英对照）
LONGDONG HONGSE GEYAO XUANYI（HANYING DUIZHAO）

译　　者　闫晓茹
出　　版　四川大学出版社
地　　址　成都市一环路南一段 24 号（610065）
发　　行　四川大学出版社
书　　号　ISBN 978-7-5690-3165-2
印前制作　四川胜翔数码印务设计有限公司
印　　刷　郫县犀浦印刷厂
成品尺寸　148mm×210mm
印　　张　12.5
字　　数　236 千字
版　　次　2019 年 11 月第 1 版
印　　次　2019 年 11 月第 1 次印刷
定　　价　49.80 元

扫码加入读者圈

◆ 读者邮购本书，请与本社发行科联系。
电话：(028)85408408/(028)85401670/
(028)86408023　邮政编码：610065
◆ 本社图书如有印装质量问题，请寄回出版社调换。
◆ 网址：http://press.scu.edu.cn

四川大学出版社
微信公众号

前　言

陇东红色歌谣是1927年至1949年流传于甘肃陇东革命根据地，反映革命斗争生活的歌谣，内容丰富，题材广泛，朗朗上口，便于传唱。唱响祖国大江南北，至今仍然经久不衰的《咱们的领袖毛泽东》《绣金匾》《军民大生产》三首革命歌曲，都诞生于甘肃陇东庆阳。这些歌谣作为老区人民的革命事业和战斗生活的重要组成部分，是老区群众昂扬向上的精神面貌和轰轰烈烈的革命斗争的真实写照。陇东红色歌谣主要以歌颂革命、歌颂共产党、歌颂人民领袖、歌颂人民军队、号召人民群众支援革命以及拥护军队为主要内容，从一种最初为自娱自乐的民间文艺形式上升成为以革命思想教育民众的主流文艺形式，在如火如荼的革命战争年代，在宣传革命道理、团结发动群众、打击敌人、丰富人民群众的文化生活方面发挥了重要作用。2006年，甘肃省人民政府将陇东红色歌谣列为第一批甘肃省非物质文化遗产。

本书翻译的陇东红色歌谣主要选自高文、巩世峰主编的《陇东红色歌谣》（甘肃人民出版社2011年6月版）一书。译者精心挑选了一百余首最能代表陇东地域特色和文化特质的革命歌谣，将其译成英语，采用汉英对照的形式，并对部分歌谣的创作背景，歌谣中的历史事件、历史人物及方言土语作了双语注释。依据歌谣的创作时期、主题诉求以及主要功能，全书分为七章，包括南梁之歌、志丹之歌、红军之歌、抗日之歌、边区之歌、解放之歌和新生活之歌。

民间歌谣是老百姓即兴而歌、口口相传的一种民间艺术形式，一般未经过刻意的雕琢与润色，所用语言较为口语化，并且包含大量的方言土语，句式整齐，押韵，平仄不严。陇东红色歌谣也不例外，其语言具有口语化的特点，通俗易懂，朗朗上口，具有浓郁的陇东乡土文化色彩，英语译文理应保留其本土特色。就文体风格而言，译文语言也应尽量口语化，通俗易懂、易记，避免使用书面语，所用词汇应为常见词汇，即用词非正式化；句中音节不能太多，句子应尽量简短精练，避免过于复杂、冗长的句式，这样才能符合陇东红色歌谣的文体特征。

20 世纪 80 年代以后，中国统一了翻译人名和地名的方法，那就是用汉语拼音翻译人名和地名，这也是目前翻译界最常用的方式，所以本书中的人名、地名基本全部采用音译（“蒋介石”姓名翻译仍然采用韦氏拼音“Chiang Kai-shek”，因其已为世界所接受）。如果原文中对重要历史事件、历史人物、重要的地名有注释，本书加以保留，并对照翻译（根据情况，译者对部分注释作了适当的修改和调整，另外，原歌谣疑有错误之处，在选入本书时也做了修改）；如果原文没有注释，必要时增加注解，适度补充，根据语境，或详或简，能对译文读者起到释难解疑的作用，在一定程度上清除了译文读者的阅读障碍。

陇东红色歌谣感情真挚，语言质朴、简单、直白、口语化，不像古诗词那样含蓄婉转，而且具有浓郁的陇东乡土气息，承载着厚重的庆阳地域文化特色。在翻译中应该讲求“信、达、雅”，既要准确传递民歌的真实含义，也要符合西方人的理解方式，即翻译家杨宪益先生主张的“忠实与通顺”。著名诗词翻译家许渊冲教授在《直译与意译》一文中指出，如果译文和原文相同的形式能表达和原文相同的内容，可以直译；反之，译文和原文相同的形式不能表达和原文相同的内容，或者虽然能表达，但是形式生硬牵强，译文读者不容易理解，那就意译。他还指出，直译和意译不能截然分开，二者应兼而用之。而且，无论直译还是意译，都要把忠实于原文的内容放在第一位。本书翻译采用异化与归化相结合、直译与意译并用的翻译策略，在语句翻译和语篇布局方面采用归化策略和英美诗歌、民歌最常见的遣词造句、谋篇构思方式，适当增词、减词、拆词、合词、正词反译，适当调整语序，前后倒置，使译文流畅地道，接受性强，有节奏感和韵律美，基本符合英语民歌语言行文规范。在词汇、修辞、形式和文化信息层面采用异化策略，尽量体现陇东红色民歌的表现手法，保留民歌语言特色，保留民歌原有民俗、文学和文化意象，使民歌保持原有韵味，以便让英语读者能领略到中国文化的多姿多彩，了解中国革命歌谣的特点和精髓，获得与汉语读者相同或类似的审美体验，以便更好地进行文化传播和交流。

毛泽东说，诗要“精练、大体整齐、押韵”。鲁迅提倡：“新诗先要有节调，押大致相近的韵，给大家容易记，又顺口，唱得出来。”许渊冲认为：“不但是写诗，译诗也该如此。”[①] 赵元任博士在《论翻译中信、达、雅的“信”的幅度》一文中写道：“译者在译诗歌时，情愿保存节律和用韵的‘信’，否则诗和歌就不伦不类了。”[②] 翻译诗词和歌谣要做到“朗朗上口”“有韵脚”“押大致相近的韵”“保存节律”，这就是诗词的“音韵美”。民歌翻译作为诗歌翻译的特殊形式，也需要注重音韵美。译文有韵脚、有节奏，读起来顺口，听起来悦耳，在韵律上与原歌谣有异曲同工之妙。诗词、歌谣文本英译时应该尽量押韵，否则原味尽失。陇东歌谣曲调多样，韵律流畅，节奏明快，抑扬有致，语言生动，朗朗上口，寓意鲜明，情感淳朴，具有浓郁的乡土气息，也具有诗词的音韵美。由于中、英两种语言在文化、语

---

① 许渊冲：《许渊冲英译〈毛泽东诗词〉》原译序，北京：中译出版社，2015 年。

② 许渊冲：《翻译的艺术（论文集）》，北京：中国对外翻译出版公司，1984 年，第 75 页。

音、语调等方面存在很大差异，歌谣翻译时要做到使译文保持与原文一样严格的韵律、音步和句数，是非常困难的。尤其是篇幅较长的歌谣，押韵难度更大。许渊冲指出，在诗词翻译实践中，即使不能完全把汉语的音律、音节美再现出来，至少应该利用英语的语音特点，比如节奏和音韵，创造出相当的“音美”来。通过使用头韵、尾韵、行内韵、近韵、谐音等，增强译文的音乐效果和节奏感，尽量做到大致押韵，尽量做到译文像诗，使其更具文学性与审美价值。在工整翻译行不通的时候，通过使用倒装求韵，在无法找到“完全押韵”的情况下“押不完全韵”或者“押近韵”，亦可模仿诗歌创作原则，像英美诗人一样，为了音韵和节奏，摆脱固有语法的约束。例如，在《刘志丹打麻鞋》这首歌谣最后一节第一行译文中（Soldier and officer were like brother），出于押尾韵需要，soldier，officer 和 brother 三个名词并未遵循传统语法规则而使用复数形式。当然，押韵要自然流畅，不能过分强求，如果为了凑韵而破坏了歌谣的意境之美，宁可不押韵，所以本书中有部分译文没有押韵。英文诗歌中常用的尾韵形式除了 aabb（双行押韵）、abab（隔行交互押韵）、abcb（隔行押韵）、abba（交错押韵）之外，还有 aaba、aaab 以及abbb等韵法。由于许多陇东歌谣原文篇幅较长（比如，《豹子川大合唱》总共 162 行），英译过程中很难用一种韵式贯穿到底，因此翻译时变韵脚、换韵式不可避免，但译文总体上押韵工整，读起来节奏感强，朗朗上口，在一定程度上传达了原文的音美。

卞之琳曾说过，诗是内容与形式高度融合的有机统一体，诗歌借形以传神，失其形即失其神。许渊冲认为“形美”可以造就“意美”。英国著名的翻译家和翻译理论家彼得·纽马克（Peter Newmark）在他的第一部著作《翻译研究途径》（*Approaches to Translation*，1981）中曾谈到翻译过程中保持原文形式的重要性，他说：“译者应注意原文的形式，用格姆布里奇的话来说，形式可以改变、提炼、表现思想。如果歪曲了原文的形式（它不可避免地总会被歪曲），就会在某种程度上歪曲了原文的思想。”① 诗词、歌谣用汉语列出来整整齐齐，译成英语有时难免就会犬牙交错。本书译者在遣词造句时有意识地控制音节长度，或省略或拆行，尽量避免句子长短不齐，使译文大体整齐，以传达汉语歌谣整齐的“外形美”。当然，如果原文长短悬殊，译文也要长短不齐，以保留汉语歌谣原有的风貌。

跨越语言的鸿沟绝非易事。民间歌谣英译是一项极具挑战性的工作，难度极大。美国诗人罗伯特·弗罗斯特（Robert Frost）曾言：“诗就是在翻译中丢失的东西。”（Poetry is what gets lost in translation.）② 写诗不易，译诗更难。翻译过程中的损益是我们必须正视的问题，翻译本身包含着矛盾——没有任何东西可以转化为它自身以外的东西。翻译尝试用一种事物解说另一种事物，注定是一场不完美的劳作，完全忠实的翻译根本不存在。要把一首诗、一首歌谣所特有的音韵、节奏、形式乃至措辞、修辞手法、神韵等用另一种语言完全对等地复制出来是不可能的。汉语诗歌、歌谣英译，不管译者如何经营，损失在所难免，这是由翻译的本质属性所决定的。

陇东红色歌谣从歌词来看，语言质朴，感情真挚，内容直白，不像诗歌那么含蓄；从曲调来看，合辙押韵，节奏感强，富有较强的音乐性。如果不考虑曲调和演唱因素，民歌歌词文本就类似于诗歌文本。在歌唱性与文学性（诗性）之间，本书翻译时更倾向于文学性，翻译成英文的歌谣便于阅读和朗诵，但很难达到演唱水平。因为，真正的艺术性的歌词翻译，应当是照顾音

① 转引自孔祥立：《“三美论”：〈红楼梦〉诗词翻译的理想标准——以许渊冲〈葬花吟〉英译为例》，载《唐山师范学院学报》，2008 年第 4 期。

② 转引自谷雨：《诗的不可译因素与不可译的诗》，载《中华读书报》，2017 年 9 月 6 日第 19 版。

乐节奏和韵脚的可以演唱的音乐文本（往往称为译配词），而本书提供的是从语义层面上翻译的文学文本，只能称为文学性翻译，是排除音乐演唱功能的翻译。

民间歌谣是地方生活的写照，是民族地域文化的传承，其质朴的语言特色、丰富的文化内涵以及独特的演唱方式都值得对其进行研究和探索。民间歌谣的翻译不仅可以丰富学术研究，而且有助于民歌走出国门，对传播民族文化具有深远的历史意义。译介是歌谣得到完好保存的方式，更是民族文化向世界传播的桥梁。陇东红色歌谣作为革命年代颇具现场感的民间创作，虽然是在“陇东”地方性的文化空间发生的，但它们却能够将地方的抗争史与国家的革命史有机地融合起来，呈现了中国现代革命的基本趋势，这就使其超越了地方性而上升为一种具有普遍意义的精神资源。陇东红色歌谣基本属于一种民间叙事形式，是老百姓用自己的语言讲述的故事，是地地道道的原生态民歌，也是中国民歌的典型代表；是劳动人民创作才能的结晶，也是真正的人民的诗。

陇东红色歌谣是红色文化和革命精神的载体，是老区革命斗争的史诗，是我国革命文化宝库中的珍品，具有较强的思想性和艺术性。它既反映了陇东人民的革命意识与革命豪情，又蕴含着浓郁的地方色彩和本土风情。陇东红色歌谣译介能够更好地对外传播中国地方民俗文化，使不同文化背景的读者有机会深入了解中国的革命道路，达到宣传南梁红色文化、弘扬陇东老区人民革命精神的目的，使“南梁精神”和红色文化走出国门，走向世界，从而实现跨文化意义上的深层次艺术化交流。本书是陇东红色歌谣汉语英译的一次大胆尝试，这种尝试也为深入保护地域性非物质文化遗产提供了一种可行的路径。

译者

2019 年 10 月

目　录
Contents

第一章　南梁之歌
Chapter One　Songs of Nanliang

南梁山水美 ······ 002
Nanliang—a beautiful place
唱南梁 ······ 004
Song of Nanliang
南梁颂 ······ 008
Ode to Nanliang
实行共产 ······ 012
Fight for communization
盼救星 ······ 014
Longing for the savior
跑！跑！跑！ ······ 016
Run！Run！Run！
游击队小唱 ······ 018
A rhyme of the guerrillas
留住游击队 ······ 020
Keeping the guerrillas in our village
一夜奔南梁 ······ 022
Going to Nanliang by night

革命有了立脚点…… 024
Nanliang—a revolutionary foothold
送哥走南梁…… 026
Seeing off my love to Nanliang
五孔窑…… 030
The five dwelling caves
南梁苏区遍地红…… 032
Nanliang Soviet Area all red
南梁政府成立了…… 034
Nanliang Soviet Government was established
光爱人民新政权…… 036
Loving but the people's new power
五哥放羊…… 038
Wu Ge—my sweet shepherd
封建制度是祸根…… 042
Cursed be the feudal system

第二章　志丹之歌
Chapter Two　Songs of Zhidan

刘志丹是好汉…… 048
A brilliant hero Liu Zhidan
南梁来了刘志丹（节选）…… 050
Liu Zhidan is come to Nanliang
刘志丹闹革命…… 052
Liu Zhidan makes a revolution
刘志丹打麻鞋…… 054
Liu Zhidan made hemp sandals

葫芦河水映红天…………………………………………………… 058
Hulu River sets aflame the skies
欢迎歇几天…………………………………………………………… 060
Welcome to stop for rest
刘志丹领导闹翻身………………………………………………… 062
Liu Zhidan leads us to make a revolution
打老谭………………………………………………………………… 064
Fighting against Lao Tan
拥护刘志丹…………………………………………………………… 070
Supporting Liu Zhidan
刘志丹………………………………………………………………… 076
Liu Zhidan
穷人跟定刘志丹…………………………………………………… 078
The poor follow none but Liu Zhidan
老刘山上喊一声…………………………………………………… 080
When Lao Liu sounds a clarion call

第三章　红军之歌

Chapter Three　Songs of the Red Army

歌唱毛主席…………………………………………………………… 084
Chanting praise of Chairman Mao
盼红军………………………………………………………………… 088
Longing for the Red Army
红军来了花不败…………………………………………………… 090
Flowers are never faded and gone
咱们的红军到南梁………………………………………………… 092
The Red Army is come to Nanliang

红军起首月明塬……………………………………… 096
The Red Army first rose in revolt in Yuemingyuan
救出千万受苦人……………………………………… 098
Saving suffering millions
红军来了穷人笑……………………………………… 100
The poor greeted the Red Army with all smiles
百姓红军一家人……………………………………… 102
The people and the Red Army are one family
找红军………………………………………………… 104
Seeking the Red Army
红旗谣………………………………………………… 106
Ballad of the red banner
红旗插上寨子湾……………………………………… 110
Red banners are waving above Zhaiziwan
红军常在咱心上……………………………………… 112
The Red Army soldiers stay in our hearts
一杆红旗空中飘……………………………………… 114
A red flag is flying on high
中央红军到陕甘……………………………………… 118
The Central Red Army is come to Shaan-Gan
红旗一展天下都红遍………………………………… 120
A red flying flag makes all around it red
当兵要当我红军……………………………………… 122
Be sure to join the Red Army
一杯酒………………………………………………… 124
A wine cup
心挨心………………………………………………… 126
Heart to heart

红旗一展天下都红遍…………………………………………………… 128
Blazing far and near when a red flag flies
咱们军民一家人……………………………………………………… 132
Army and people are family
我们是红军的武装…………………………………………………… 134
We are the forces of the Red Army

第四章　抗日之歌
Chapter Four　Songs of Resistance Against Japan

我们的天地…………………………………………………………… 138
Our heaven and earth
上前线………………………………………………………………… 140
Starting for the front
送兵…………………………………………………………………… 142
Seeing my dearest off to the front
玩花灯………………………………………………………………… 144
Watching lantern shows
新三恨歌……………………………………………………………… 148
A new song of three hates
劝当兵………………………………………………………………… 152
To be a soldier
做针线………………………………………………………………… 156
Doing needlework
拥军歌………………………………………………………………… 160
Song of supporting the army
飞针走线做鞋忙……………………………………………………… 164
Busy with shoe sewing

人民救星人民爱…… 166
The people's beloved savior
八路军真正好…… 168
To the Eighth Route Army our praise shall be
做军鞋…… 172
Sewing shoes for soldiers
四季歌…… 182
Song of four seasons
十杯酒…… 184
A toast song
留守兵团军歌…… 190
The military song of the left-behind regiment
生产谣（节选）…… 194
Ballad of production (Excerpt)
自卫军…… 198
Self-defense corps
大凤川…… 200
Dafengchuan
抗日军政大学校歌…… 202
Song of Anti-Japanese Military and Political College of China
春天歌…… 206
Song of spring
抗大七分校校歌…… 208
Song of the Seventh Branch School of Kangda
春天百花歌…… 212
When the spring breaks into flowers
纺线线…… 214
Spinning threads

开荒曲…………………………………………………………… 216
Ballad of reclamation
缴公粮…………………………………………………………… 218
Delivery of tax grain

第五章 边区之歌

Chapter Five Songs of the Border Region

边区就是咱的家……………………………………………… 222
The border region is our home
毛主席像太阳…………………………………………………… 224
Chairman Mao is like the red sun
我们边区像清泉………………………………………………… 226
Our border region is like a clear spring
我们边区团结得像铁桶………………………………………… 230
Closely united are our border region men
文教大会歌……………………………………………………… 232
Song of education
自己动手建学校 ……………………………………………… 234
We build schools ourselves
放脚歌…………………………………………………………… 236
Song of unbinding the feet
绣荷包…………………………………………………………… 238
Making an embroidered pouch
边区好…………………………………………………………… 242
The border region is a nice place
选举歌…………………………………………………………… 244
Song of election

玩花灯…………………………………………………… 246
Parading lighted lanterns
穷人翻身乐哈哈…………………………………………… 250
The liberated poor beam with smiles
太阳出来照地红…………………………………………… 252
The rising sun shines the earth red
闹变工…………………………………………………… 254
Labor exchange
军民大生产………………………………………………… 260
The great production of the Army and the people
军民大生产………………………………………………… 264
The great production of the Army and the people
军民大生产………………………………………………… 268
The great production of the Army and the people
十绣金匾…………………………………………………… 272
The golden banner with ten embroideries
绣金匾……………………………………………………… 282
Embroidering the golden banner
绣金匾……………………………………………………… 286
Embroidering the golden banner
五枝花……………………………………………………… 290
Five flowers
毛主席号召大生产 ……………………………………… 294
Chairman Mao calls on us to promote production

第六章　解放之歌
Chapter Six　Songs of Liberation

准备打胜仗………………………………………………… 300
Ready to fight for victory

毛主席领导咱打江山…… 302
Chairman Mao leads us to fight for a new life
毛主席举旗向前进…… 304
Chairman Mao leads us onward
送夫参军…… 306
Sending my loving husband into the army
送公粮…… 310
Deliver tax grain to the front
拥军小唱…… 312
Song of supporting the army
解放小调…… 314
A ditty of liberation
革命成了功…… 316
The revolution ends in victory
牧童歌…… 318
Song of a shepherd boy
豹子川大合唱…… 320
A chorus Baozichuan makes
陇东中学校歌…… 338
Song of Longdong Middle School
我们的歌…… 342
Song of ours

第七章　新生活之歌

Chapter Seven　Songs of New Life

生产小调…… 348
A ditty of production

国庆小唱 …… 350
Song of National Day
毛主席是咱的大救星 …… 354
Chairman Mao is our big savior
人民心向共产党 …… 356
The people are true to the Communist Party
农忙十二月 …… 358
Busy all year long with agricultural work
献上颂歌献上心 …… 364
Singing songs with our hearts
五哥放羊唱新曲 …… 368
Wu Ge a shepherd boy sings a new song
新唱《绣金匾》 …… 370
A new version of *Embroidering the Golden Banner*

参考文献 …… 374
后　记 …… 378

第一章
Chapter One

南梁之歌
Songs of Nanliang

南梁[①]山水美

山数南梁的美，
水数南梁的甜，
绿茵茵梢山望不断，
清泠泠流水亮闪闪。

---

① 南梁，地名，今华池县南梁乡、林镇乡、山庄乡等地，与合水县及陕西志丹、吴起、甘泉等县接壤。刘志丹在渭华起义失败后，即在这一带发动游击战争，是陕甘边区根据地中心区域。1934 年 11 月 7 日，在这里成立了习仲勋任主席的陕甘边区苏维埃政府（简称南梁政府），刘志丹任军委主席。南梁是当时陕甘边区党政军领导机关的所在地。

Nanliang[①]—a beautiful place

No hills are beautiful as those in Nanliang,
No waters taste sweet as those in Nanliang,
The endless greens continuing and stretching,
The crystal clear rivers flowing and glistening.

---

① Nanliang, a place name, now includes such townships as Nanliang, Linzhen and Shanzhuang of Huachi County, bordering on Heshui County and the counties of Zhidan, Wuqi and Ganquan in Shaanxi Province. After the fall of Weihua Uprising, Liu Zhidan fought guerrilla warfare in Nanliang, which was the center area of the revolutionary base of the Shaanxi-Gansu Border Region. On November 7, 1934 the Soviet Government of the Shaanxi-Gansu Border Region (also known as Nanliang government) was brought into being with Xi Zhongxun as the Chairman and Liu Zhidan as the Chairman of the Military Commission. Nanliang was the site for the Shaanxi-Gansu Border Region leading bodies of the Party, the Government and the Army at that time.

唱南梁

山丹丹花开红堂堂，
缅怀先烈唱南梁，
自从来了共产党，
劳苦人民得解放，
得呀得解放。

山丹丹花开红堂堂，
缅怀先烈唱南梁，
刘志丹来习仲勋[①]，
领导咱们变模样，
变呀变模样。

① 习仲勋，陕甘红军和陕甘边区革命根据地的创建者和领导人之一。曾任中共陕甘边区特委军委书记，陕甘边区革命委员会副主席、主席，陕甘边区苏维埃政府主席等职务，为开创照金根据地、南梁根据地乃至陕甘宁边区抗日民主根据地做出了重要贡献。

Song of Nanliang

Flaming as fire morningstar lilies are in full bloom,
We sing of Nanliang to remember martyrs in gloom.
Since the Communist Party is here come,
The suffering people liberated become,
Liberated and liberated become.

Flaming as fire morningstar lilies are in full bloom,
We sing of Nanliang to remember martyrs in gloom.
Both Liu Zhidan and Xi Zhongxun①
Take us to fight for a better world,
A better and better world.

---

① Xi Zhongxun was one of the founders and leaders of the Shaanxi-Gansu Red Army and the revolutionary base area in the Shaan-Gan Border Region. He acted as the Military Secretary of the Special Committee in the Shaan-Gan Border Region, Vice Chairman and Chairman of the Shaan-Gan Border Region Revolutionary Committee, and also Chairman of the Shaan-Gan Border Region Soviet Government. He made great contributions to the establishment of Zhaojin revolutionary base area, Nanliang revolutionary base area and the Anti-Japanese democratic base area in the Shaan-Gan-Ning Border Region.

山丹丹花开红堂堂，
缅怀先烈唱南梁，
先烈开拓阳关道，
改革开放奔小康，
奔呀奔小康。

山丹丹花开红堂堂，
缅怀先烈唱南梁，
红色传统继承好，
建设和谐新庆阳，
建设呀新庆阳。

Flaming as fire morningstar lilies are in full bloom,
We sing of Nanliang to remember martyrs in gloom.
The martyred men have blazed a bright way,
Reform and opening up bring us a good life today,
A good and good life today.

Flaming as fire morningstar lilies are in full bloom,
We sing of Nanliang to remember martyrs in gloom.
Let's keep and carry the fine red traditions on,
To build a new and harmonious Qingyang,
A new and harmonious Qingyang.

南梁颂

山数南梁的青，
水数南梁的甜。
南梁连着井冈山，
华池浪涌延河川。
绿茵茵青山走千里，
清泠泠春水流万年。

山数南梁的美，
水数南梁的滟。
南梁林海红星闪，
星火燎原换新天。
脆生生欢歌传千里，
红彤彤旗帜飘万年。

山数南梁的高，
水数南梁的暖。
南梁山水育群英，

Ode to Nanliang

No hills are greener than those in Nanliang,
No waters taste sweeter than those in Nanliang.
Nanliang is linked in spirit to Jinggangshan,
Huachi has surged its waves into Yanhechuan.
Green mountains stretch for mile after mile,
Sparkling streams flow on year after year.

No hills are as beauteous as those in Nanliang,
No waters as glistening as those in Nanliang.
Red stars shine bright above the green trees anew,
A little spark kindles a great fire to make skies new.
Sweet songs of joy drift on for miles and miles,
And red banners flutter high for years and years.

No mountains are higher than those in Nanliang,
No waters feel warmer than those in Nanliang.
Nanliang's rills and hills breed a host of heroes,

艰苦奋斗捷报传。

一代代英才创新业，

一辈辈新人勇向前。

Hard work brings reports of good news in showers.
Generations of brilliant talents create greater glories,
And generations of youth bravely march on forwards.

实行共产[①]

连年大旱，天逼民反；
苛捐杂税，官逼民反；
若要不反，离死不远；
大家起来，实行共产。

① 这首歌谣据传是1929年冬至1930年春，刘志丹在华池县（时属庆阳县）南梁、林镇、二将川等地发动贫苦农民奋起开展革命斗争时所作，在南梁山区广为传唱。

Fight for communization[①]

Years of drought, heaven drives people to revolt;
Taxes and levies, officials drive people to revolt;
With no resistance, we are all doomed to die out;
Let's rise in revolution, fight for communization.

---

① It is said that Liu Zhidan created this revolutionary folk song during the period from the winter of 1929 to the spring of 1930 when he mobilized the poor peasants to rise in revolution in Nanliang, Linzhen and Erjiangchuan of Huachi County (then Qingyang County). It then achieved widespread popularity throughout the Nanliang mountain areas.

盼救星

盼星星，盼月亮，
穷人盼的共产党，
共产党来救星来，
穷人翻身见太阳。

Longing for the savior

Day long, night long, the poor here
Long for the Communist Party dear,
For the Party to the poor is a savior,
Who helps them rise up to the light.

跑！跑！跑！

跑跑跑，快快跑，
豪绅头上是目标，
拿起斧，拿起刀，
要杀掉呀么要杀掉。

工农联合心一条，
大家齐心向前跑，
地主、豪绅、军阀、官僚，
铲除掉呀么铲除掉。

Run! Run! Run!

Run, run, run, run faster,
Run to chase the tyrants.
Take up swords and spears,
Smite once, and smite no more.

Unite closely workers and peasants,
With one heart we march on forwards.
Tyrants, bureaucrats, landlords and warlords,
All will be wiped out, and will be wiped out.

游击队小唱

天当房，

地当床，

星月作灯光，

草地暖心房。

A rhyme of the guerrillas

With the sky for our house,
The earth serving as bed,
And the moon and stars lights,
The meadow warms our hearts.

留住游击队

留住游击队，
住在咱庄上。
亲人在，
有爹又有娘。
亲人走了，
来虎又来狼。

Keeping the guerrillas in our village

Ask the guerrillas
To garrison our village.
When they are here,
Good guards we have.
When they are away,
Wolves and tigers, instead.

一夜奔南梁

一轮月儿亮堂堂，
照咱哥哥把路上。
哥哥逃离财主家，
出笼的鸟儿展翅翔。
过了河来上山冈，
一夜投奔到南梁。
头包毛巾手持枪，
要和财主算细账。

Going to Nanliang by night

A silver moon beams bright high above,
Illuminating the trail for my dear love.
Winging wildly out of the cage like a bird,
He finally flies away from the landlord.
Going across rivers, climbing over ridges,
After a night's toil, he's come to Nanliang.
With head wrapped in towel, gun in hand,
Old scores will he settle with the landlord.

革命有了立脚点

南梁堡子大梢山，
陕甘交界两不管。
刘志丹，看得远，
带领红军上梢山。

扫清土匪和民团，
占据梢山扎营盘。
革命有了立脚点，
武装割据陕甘边。

Nanliang—a revolutionary foothold

Bosomed in green hills, dotted with fortresses,
Nanliang sits in limbo 'tween the two provinces[①].
Liu Zhidan, a military officer who's far-sighted,
Deep into the mountains the Red Army guided.

With civil corps and bandits off finished,
Spreading banner he set up the stronghold.
Nanliang became a revolutionary foothold,
And a Separatist Regime thus established.

---

① The two provinces refer to Shaanxi and Gansu.

送哥走南梁

鸡叫三遍天快亮，
情哥一心走南梁，
百里去寻共产党，
小妹送哥把路上。

送哥送到五里坡，
手拉手儿叫哥哥，
革命意志要坚决，
一心杀敌莫想我。

送哥送到十里墩，
送上个荷包表妹心，
荷包虽小情意深，
盼你立功传喜讯。

Seeing off my love to Nanliang

At the cock's third crow, bright the day grows,
With an iron will to Nanliang my beloved goes
For the Communist Party a hundred miles away,
And here I come to see my dear start on the way.

I accompany my sweetheart to Wulipo,
Hand in hand we go, I tell my beloved,
"A strong revolutionary will you'd hold,
In the fight you must be brave and bold."

When sending my beloved to Shilidun,
I tell him, "Take this self-made pouch
As a token of my eternal love for you,
And I expect a message of your merit, too."

送哥送过浪子河[1]，
隔河扬手喊哥哥，
妹妹就爱红军哥，
十年八年我等着。

① 浪子河在华池与庆阳（今庆城）交界处。

Until seeing him off over the Langzi River[①],
I wave goodbye to my dear across the river,
"I love nobody but you, my dear soldier lover,
However long it takes I'll wait for you forever."

① The Langzi River runs through the border area between Huachi County and Qingyang County (now Qingcheng County).

五孔窑[1]

喝的山泉水，
吃的糜子饭，
睡的五孔窑，
穿的羊毛毡。
上山去种地，
下山把书念，
敌人来“围剿”，
勒马[2]和他干。

---

① 五孔窑：指的是刘志丹创办的陕甘边区军政干部学校所在地的五孔窑洞，故址在今华池县林镇乡张岔村。

② 陇东方言，立刻，立即。

The five dwelling caves[①]

Drink water from the fountain,
Eat meals of millet on the mountain.
Live in the five dwelling caves,
And wear felted wool coats.
Go up the mountain to farm,
And down the mountain to read.
If the enemies dare to attack,
In no time we'll beat them back.

① The five dwelling caves were located in the village of Zhangcha of Linzhen Township in Huachi County. There stood the Shaan-Gan Border Region Military-political Cadres School established by Liu Zhidan.

南梁苏区遍地红

红布条条胸前挂，
一把马刀腰间挎。
跟上志丹闹革命，
一心革命打天下。

长矛磨得闪闪亮，
马刀飞快映红绫。
四面八方打土豪，
南梁苏区遍地红。

Nanliang Soviet Area all red

A piece of red cloth on the chest,
And a saber is worn at the waist.
Follow Zhidan to make a revolution,
And free our land with resolution.

Brightly sparkling are long spears,
Red tassels radiant on sharp sabers.
Local tyrants we fight here and there,
Nanliang Soviet Area is red everywhere.

南梁政府成立了

天黑地黑暗无光，
不分东西南北方。
南梁来了刘志丹，
志丹宣传共产党。
南梁政府成立了，
穷人掌权硬邦邦。
志丹领头咱们上，
分了土地分牛羊。

Nanliang Soviet Government was established

When gloomy above and dark below,
We got lost for none we could follow.
And yet at Nanliang Liu Zhidan arrived,
He got the Communist Party publicized.
With Nanliang Soviet government founded,
The poor people seized power as desired.
Zhidan, our guide, took us to be liberated,
With cattle distributed and land allocated.

光爱人民新政权

不爱银子不爱财，
光爱工农苏维埃；
不爱金子不爱钱，
光爱人民新政权。

Loving but the people's new power

We love neither silver nor property,
But the Workers' and Peasants' Soviet;
We crave neither gold nor money,
But the people's new political power.

五哥放羊

正月里来正月正，
家家户户玩花灯，
公鸡叫鸣天麻亮，
五哥放羊去上工。

东家财主真狠心，
他把五哥不当人，
整日放羊吃不饱，
放羊回来又担粪。

六月里来三伏天，
五哥放羊在高山，
手里只拿放羊鞭，
大雨淋透破衣衫。

蹚过河来爬上山，
给我五哥送雨伞，
五哥人穷心肠好，
至死爱他心不变。

Wu Ge—my sweet shepherd

In the first month of the lunar year,
Red lanterns hang over every gate.
When a cock crows, it is dark still,
Wu Ge has to go herding on the hill.

The landlord has a heart cruel and cold ever,
And sees Wu Ge as a human being never.
He keeps his sheep on an empty stomach all day,
And carries manure when he comes back alway.

In lunar June come the hottest days of the year,
Deep in the mountain Wu Ge keeps his sheep.
Holding nothing in hand but a shepherd's whip,
In a heavy storm in rags he's soaked to the skin.

Across the river and up the hill,
I bring my Wu Ge an umbrella.
Poor as he is, yet kind and pure,
And thus my love for him will endure.

八月里来秋风凉，
我给五哥缝衣裳，
缝上一件小棉袄，
送给五哥御寒凉。

十月里来寒冷天，
五哥拦羊在深山，
身披毡袄迎风站，
两眼哭得泪不干。

来了救星共产党，
把咱百姓都解放，
穷人翻身自做主，
我和五哥配成双。

A cool autumn wind rises as lunar August comes near,
I sew clothes for Wu Ge, my shepherd dear.
Padded with cotton I've made a small coat,
Given to my love as a defense against the cold.

In lunar October when the weather turns chill,
Wu Ge still keeps his sheep deep in the hill.
Shivering against the wind in a thin coat,
He sheds tear on tear all day in the cold.

Here comes the Communist Party, the savior,
Who has saved and liberated all the poor.
We're now risen up to breathe the free air,
Wu Ge and I finally make a perfect, happy pair.

封建制度是祸根

封建压迫几千年，
咱们妇女实可怜，
三四岁上把脚缠下，
疼得人儿难动弹。

可叹咱们妇女家，
从小就要守家法，
长大成家不由自己，
父母卖咱当牛马。

一天围着锅台转，
夜里推磨到二更天，
起床等不得鸡叫唤，
光学会个抱娃娃。

丈夫打来公婆骂，
人前头做事没有咱，

Cursed be the feudal system

Feudal oppression ran through thousand years,
We women, so poor, so long, shed bitter tears.
At three or four we had had our feet bound,
There stirred quite a pain that we hardly got around.

Alas! Alack! Women heaved sighs deep and long,
When young, we obeyed but the family rules strong;
Grown up, we had no liberty to choose the bridegroom,
Parents simply sold us to men as slaves in full bloom.

We were merely confined to housework,
Getting up before the crow of the cock,
Grinding grain into flour till midnight hour,
And looking after our kids in the bower.

All the time we had to be secluded from public view,
Neither whipped by men nor scolded by in-laws were few.

说话不敢把牙齿露，
走路不敢抬起头。

男人女人都是人，
为啥男女不平等，
恨爹恨娘不顶用，
封建制度是祸根。

晴天响起一声雷，
组织起妇女联合会，
齐心推翻三座山，
妇女们才能把身翻。

妇女们婚姻自由了，
自己对象自己找，
相亲相爱甜如蜜，
再不受那旁人的气。

We ventured not to show our teeth while speaking,
Nor did we dare to heave our heads while walking.

Both males and females are human beings,
But why did women enjoy no equal rights?
Blame neither Dad nor Mom, for it's no use,
'Tis on the feudal system that lays the curse.

A thunder rolls loud across the clear sky,
Women's Unions have been formed far and nigh.
The Chinese women can not win liberation
Unless we topple the Three Mountains with resolution.

Now we've won our freedom and pride,
No more shall others over us ride.
We look for spouses by ourselves,
And the love of a fond pair is sweet as honey.

第二章

Chapter Two

志丹之歌

Songs of Zhidan

刘志丹[1]是好汉

刘志丹，是好汉，
精脚片子[2]打裹缠，
腰里别[3]的手榴弹，
断[4]的白军跑不绊[5]。

刘志丹，是好汉，
不拿架子满和善，
半月二十常见面，
和咱老乡好熟惯。

---

① 刘志丹，名景桂，字子丹、志丹。中国工农红军高级将领，陕甘红军和陕甘边区革命根据地的主要创建人和领导人之一。1930 年至 1935 年，刘志丹率领南梁游击队、陕甘红军转战陇东的华池、合水、宁县、正宁、庆阳、环县等地，为创建以南梁为中心的陕甘边区革命根据地进行了英勇斗争。

② 陇东方言，光着脚。

③ 陇东方言，插。

④ 陇东方言，追赶。

⑤ 陇东方言，跑不及。

A brilliant hero Liu Zhidan①

Liu Zhidan is a hero brave and bold,
With feet bare, legs half wrapped,
And hand-grenades on the waist belt,
His chase the White Army② never escaped.

Liu Zhidan is a hero of noble mind,
With no airs but a heart kind.
He sees or meets us at intervals,
And thus a dear friend of our locals.

---

① Liu Zhidan took the name of Jinggui and the style of Zhidan. He was a high-ranking officer of the Chinese Workers' and Peasants' Red Army, and one of the founders and leaders of the Shaanxi-Gansu Red Army and the Shaanxi-Gansu Border Region revolutionary base. From 1930 to 1935, Liu Zhidan led the Nanliang guerillas and the Shaanxi-Gansu Red Army to fight brave battles in such counties of Longdong as Huachi, Heshui, Ningxian, Zhengning, Qingyang and Huanxian to establish the Shaanxi-Gansu Border Region revolutionary base centered on Nanliang.

② The White Army here refers to the military army of Kuomintang during the first Chinese Civil War from 1927 to 1937.

南梁来了刘志丹（节选）

（一）

日头出来端上端，
南梁来了刘志丹，
志丹练兵又宣传，
要把世事颠倒颠。

（二）

自南梁来了刘志丹，
咱们的日子不一般。
打倒了土豪和老财，
打翻了军阀和赃官。
没地的农民有了地，
没穿的穷人有了穿。
自己动手来自己吃，
再没有杂税和苛捐。

Liu Zhidan is come to Nanliang

I

Just to the mid sky the sun rises,
At Nanliang arrives Liu Zhidan,
He trains troops, folks mobilizes,
To turn the world upside down.

II

Since Liu Zhidan is come to Nanliang,
Our life is not as it was in the days old.
Destroyed are all the bullies and landlords,
Overthrown corrupt officials and warlords.
The farmers have seized back their deprived land,
And the poor in want of clothes are now well-clad.
With our brain and muscle, well-fed now we are,
No heavy taxes and levies imposed on us there are.

刘志丹闹革命

东面山来西面山，
陕北出了个刘志丹。
刘志丹出来闹革命，
领导工农打江山。

Liu Zhidan makes a revolution

Mountain in the east and mountain in the west,
Northern Shaanxi has brought forth a Liu Zhidan,
Who comes out just to make the revolution,
Leading workers and peasants to seize power with resolution.

刘志丹打麻鞋

陕甘游击队，
老谢总指挥，
领兵上陕北呀，
打保安失败回[①]。

退在墩儿梁[②]，
敌兵来撵上，
撵住打一仗呀，
两家都没伤。

夜住麻地台[③]，
士兵没鞋穿，

---

① 指 1932 年秋谢子长、刘志丹率领中国工农红军陕甘游击队攻打保安县（今志丹县）失利。

② 墩儿梁是位于华池县、合水县和陕西省志丹县交界处的一座山梁。

③ 麻地台在华池县和志丹县接界的地方。

Liu Zhidan made hemp sandals

The Shaanxi-Gansu guerrillas
Took Lao Xie as a commander.
He led troops to Northern Shaanxi,
Yet defeated in the Battle of Baoan①.

While retreating to Dunerliang②,
They were closely pursued by the foes,
And then forced to put up a fierce fight,
However, with injuries on each side light.

In Maditai③ Village they spent the night,
For soldiers had no shoes to wear right,

---

① In the autumn of 1932, Xie Zichang and Liu Zhidan lost the battle when they led the Shaanxi-Gansu guerrillas to attack Baoan County (now Zhidan County).

② Dunerliang is a mountain ridge on the border of the three counties—Huachi, Heshui of Qingyang and Zhidan in Shaanxi Province.

③ Maditai is on the border of the two counties of Huachi and Zhidan.

老刘坐灯下呀，
连夜打麻鞋。

麻鞋打成了，
老刘忙做饭，
士兵睡醒来呀，
热饭摆面前。

官兵同甘苦，
好比亲兄弟，
失败不灰心呀，
齐心杀敌人。

Lao Liu sat in the flickering lamp light,
Making hemp sandals that very night.

When done were the sandals,
Lao Liu started to cook meals.
When from sleep rose the soldiers,
Hot food was ready on the tables.

Soldier and officer were like brother,
Weal and woe they shared with each other.
When beaten in battle, they lost heart never,
Yet still side by side fought the foes as ever.

葫芦河水映红天

葫芦河，弯又弯，
河边住着刘志丹，
老刘住了没三年，
葫芦河水映红天。

Hulu River sets aflame the skies

The winding Hulu River glides,
By the shore Liu Zhidan abides.
For no more than three years,
The river sets aflame the skies.

欢迎歇几天[①]

陕北游击队，
老谢总指挥；
打开安定县，
犯人放出监；
下到南梁堡，
见了刘志丹；
老刘亲热说，
欢迎歇几天。

① 这首民歌唱的是1934年7月下旬谢子长率领陕北游击队主力来到南梁根据地时，受到南梁军民热烈欢迎的情景。

Welcome to stop for rest[1]

The Northern Shaanxi guerrillas
Took Lao Xie as a commander;
With Anding County liberated,
Victims in jail were emancipated;
When down to Nanliangbu Village,
The gueriIlas met Liu Zhidan,
Who, in a glowing tone, said,
"Welcome to stop for rest."

① This ballad faithfully records how the main force of the Northern Shaanxi guerrillas led by Xie Zichang was warmly welcomed by the people and the army at Nanliang revolutionary base when they arrived there in late July 1934.

刘志丹领导闹翻身

前梁梁糜子后梁梁谷，
刘志丹领导咱闹翻身。

山尖尖一面面红旗飘，
打土豪分田地为咱穷人好。

山里头打仗山外头红，
闹起了革命才翻了身。

叫声娃娃你快去从军，
刘志丹是咱领路的人。

Liu Zhidan leads us to make a revolution

Millet on the front ridges, sorghum on the back ones,
To make revolutions Liu Zhidan takes the poor ones.

Waving atop high mountains are the banners bright,
Overthrowing tyrants and allocating land, we see light.

Battles inside the mountain make the outside red,
We can't be free till revolutions have been spread.

Hurry to join the army, guys from far and wide,
For we have Liu Zhidan who serves as our guide.

打老谭

民国乱哄哄，
出了个谭世麟①，
他是民团的头，
清乡的总司令。

谭贼真可恨，
元城川他占定，
逼粮款又拉兵，
苦害老百姓。

谭贼真是凶，
无恶他不行，

---

① 谭世麟（1879—1951），庆城人。1927 年起任国民党陇东民团军总司令、清乡司令，惯用刀铡、斧砍、活埋等酷刑残杀共产党员及无辜群众，搜刮民财无数。1950 年，在华池县柔远城被判处死刑，就地枪决。

Fighting against Lao Tan[1]

Riots broke out in the Republic of China,
Where there brought forth a Tan Shilin[2],
Who was the head of civil corps and
Commander of the country-clearing band.

Devil Tan was vicious as he could,
And Yuanchengchuan he occupied;
Taxes levied and conscripts seized,
He was guilty of the people's plight.

Devil Tan was atrocious as he could,
There was no evil he never did.

---

① Lao Tan here refers to Tan Shilin, see note 2 in detail.

② Tan Shilin (1879 – 1951) was born in Qingcheng County. He was the commander-in-chief of Longdong civil corps of Kuomintang and the commander of the country-clearing band during the Second Civil War. He used to savage the Red Army soldiers, communists and innocent civilians with such tools as chaff-cutters and axes, and such cruel means as burying alive. He also looted the common people's properties untold. In 1950, he was sentenced to death and shot on the spot in Rouyuan, Huachi County.

大路口安铜铡，
铡的是穷人。

半夜打了个闪，
来了刘志丹，
他带上游击队，
一心要打老谭[1]。

红军出了营，
随带上娃娃兵[2]，
游击队来赤卫军，
打仗为老百姓。

来在兰沟门[3]，
堡子包围定，
老百姓都上阵，
围了个不透风。

---

① 1935年初，红二十六军四十二师的红三团和抗日义勇军，歼灭谭部盘踞华池县五蛟堡的一个连。当地老百姓传唱这次战斗是刘志丹指挥，实际是由王世泰和郭宝珊二人指挥的。

② 娃娃兵，指刘志丹在红军和游击队组建的少年先锋队。

③ 兰沟门是五蛟堡下一个村庄名。

At the cross-road he set a copper hay-cutter,
Which was expressly intended for the poor.

A bolt of lightening flashed at midnight cold,
Here came Liu Zhidan,
Who, with the guerilla soldiers bold,
Was well prepared to fight Lao Tan①.

Out of the camp rushed the red fighters,
Closely followed by the child soldiers②,
The Red Guards as well as the guerillas,
They all fought a fight for the civilians.

When reaching the village of Langoumen,
All the fighters, in a flash, laid siege to the fort.
Villagers also engaged in it from far and wide,
And encompassed Tan's camp on every side.

---

① Early in 1935, the 3rd regiment from the 42nd division of the 26th Red Army group and the anti-Japanese volunteers overcame one company of Tan's civil corps entrenched in Wujiaobu in Huachi County. The local people took for granted that this battle was directed by Liu Zhidan; however, it was actually commanded by Wang Shitai and Guo Baoshan.

② Child soldiers refer to young pioneers organized by Liu Zhidan in the Red Army and the guerillas.

断水又断粮，
谭贼着了忙，
他带团要逃跑，
红军紧追上。

王桥[1]打一仗，
民团解决光，
老百姓哈哈笑，
堡子打开了。

刘志丹真英雄，
除害为百姓，
穷人都要跟他走，
闹呀闹革命。

① 王桥在华池县五蛟乡境内，距离五蛟堡十余里。

With neither food nor water,
Devil Tan was a lot hotter
That he took flight with his followers,
But close behind ran the Red Army soldiers.

At Wangqiao[①] a fight broke out,
With the civil corps wiped out.
The folks grinned from ear to ear,
For the fort was finally opened sheer.

Liu Zhidan proved to be a real hero,
Who helped rid the people of an evil.
All the poor followed him with resolution
To make, make the revolution.

① Wangqiao is located in Wujiao Township of Huachi County, more than 5 kilometers from Wujiaobu.

拥护刘志丹

半夜里来叫门，
问你是哪部分，
只要说是老刘的，
赶快迎进门。

哪里有老刘，
哪里人最稠，
男女老少都围满，
话儿拉不够。

喂马有咱们，
放哨有咱们，
老刘的队伍快缓好[1]，
打仗有精神。

① 陇东方言，休息好。

Supporting Liu Zhidan

When you knock at a gate late at night,
You'll be asked in which column you fight.
If you say you're under Lao Liu's command,
Warmly in the house you'll be welcomed.

Where there is Lao Liu,
There are more people.
Men and women, young and old,
Cheerful chatting knows no end.

Horses we feed,
And sentry we stand.
Lao Liu's army takes a rest day and night
That the soldiers are keen to fight.

哪里有白军，
女人乱逃奔；
老刘的队伍开到了，
妇女来欢迎。

送来大西瓜，
送来鞋和袜，
还有一捧捧大红枣，
亲人请收下。

请吃猪羊肉，
请吃热馍馍，
老刘喜欢吃荞面，
赶快压饸饹。

红军要开走，
人人都挽留，
拉住老刘的左右手，
左右[①]不让走。

老刘呀大恩人，
老刘呀救命星，

① 左右，这里是说什么也不行的意思。

Where the White Army soldiers appear,
Women flee in all directions with fear.
However, when Lao Liu's army has come,
Women give them a warm welcome.

Bring big watermelons,
Bring shoes and socks,
And handfuls of big dates sweet,
They urge our dear soldiers to eat.

Serve meat and mutton,
Serve hot steamed bread,
And cook buckwheat noodles in haste,
When they know 'tis Lao Liu's favorite.

When the Red Army soldiers depart,
With them none would like to part.
No matter what Lao Liu says, oh,
They clasp his hands and never let go.

Lao Liu is a big benefactor,
Lao Liu is a big liberator.

全凭你领导闹革命，
穷人才翻身。

土地呀有土地，
牛羊呀有牛羊，
全凭你领导闹革命，
咱们把家当。

自由呀多自由，
平等呀真平等，
全凭你领导闹革命，
才有好光景。

On you our hopes fix for the revolution
That the poor win liberty and liberation.

Land we have,
Cattle and sheep we have.
On you our hopes fix for the revolution
That we make the masters of our nation.

Liberty we have,
Equality we have.
On you our hopes fix for the revolution
That we've lived in a good condition.

刘志丹

正月里来是新年，
陕北出了个刘志丹。
刘志丹真勇敢，
他带队伍上横山，
一心要共产。

二月里来刮春风，
江西上来个毛泽东。
毛泽东来真威风，
他带的红军势力重，
就有百万兵。

三月里来三月三，
如今的世道大改变，
男当红军女宣传，
走起路来实好看，
人人都称赞。

Liu Zhidan

As the first moon celebrates the happy New Year,
Northern Shaanxi has brought forth a Liu Zhidan.
Bold and brave is Liu Zhidan,
Who leads his men up Mount Hengshan,
With an iron will to destroy the despot.

The vernal wind blows in the second moon,
Jiangxi has brought forth a Mao Zedong.
Powerful and prestigious is Mao Zedong,
Who leads a great army of Red soldiers,
They're all gallant and valiant warriors.

On the third day of the third moon it be,
Ah! What great changes of today we see!
Men are Red soldiers, women loudspeakers,
They all walk with vigorous strides,
In every heart praise abides.

穷人跟定刘志丹

陕甘高原山连山，
穷人跟定刘志丹。
男当红军女宣传，
娃娃组织儿童团。

山连水来水连山，
老刘穷人心相连。
斗倒地主分田产，
陕甘高原红了天。

The poor follow none but Liu Zhidan

Hills upon hills on the plateau of Shaan-Gan,
The poor will follow nobody but Liu Zhidan.
Men are Red soldiers, women loudspeakers,
Children are members of the Children's corps.

Back to back the mountains and the rivers lie,
Heart to heart Lao Liu and the poor are linked.
With landlords destroyed and land distributed,
The sky over the Shaan-Gan plateau blazes red.

老刘山上喊一声

南梁山上插红旗，
映红陕甘山和水。
老刘山上喊一声，
遍地穷人都响应。

放羊娃娃揽工汉，
争相报名把军参。
红军是咱大救星，
要想翻身当红军。

When Lao Liu sounds a clarion call

High above Nanliang the red flags are flapping,
The mountains and rivers in Shaan-Gan flaming.
When Lao Liu sounds a clarion call for revolution,
Near and far the poor rise in response with resolution.

Shepherds and farmhands,
All rush to join the army.
The Red Army is our savior,
To rise up is to be a Red soldier.

第三章
Chapter Three

红军之歌
Songs of the Red Army

歌唱毛主席

南京到北京，
哪一个不闻名，
中国的领袖，
就是毛泽东，
领导咱们大翻身，
咱们的大救星。

毛主席他一来，
衙门大敞开，
谁有苦来谁有冤，
一起吐出来，
打倒土豪大恶霸，
穷人把头抬。

毛主席好领导，

Chanting praise of Chairman Mao

From Nanjing to Beijing,
None knows not
The leader of China
Is Mao Zedong.
He is our great liberator,
Who steers us to liberation.

When Chairman Mao comes here,
The Yamen[①] gates open wide far and near.
Those, grievously wronged,
Pour out their heart with bitterness thronged.
Down with bullies and landlords,
The poor people lift their heads.

Chairman Mao is a good leader of foresight,

① Yamen: government office in feudal China.

天下尽清官，
他一心为百姓，
赛过活神仙，
边区办得呱呱叫，
一片好河山。

毛主席订计划，
遍地开红花，
老百姓掌大权，
再不受欺压，
自己的事情自己管，
人民坐天下。

With officials and officers honest and upright.
He works for the people heart and hand,
Like immortals they live on the land.
The border region of mountain and river
Has been so flourishing never!

Chairman Mao maps out brilliant programmes,
Whose powers crown the land with red flowers.
The people have now possessed political power,
Free from exploitation and oppression forever.
We're now the lords and owners of our own fate,
And our people become the masters of the state.

盼红军

种下庄稼盼收成，
穷人日夜盼红军，
红军来了打豪绅，
仇要报来怨要伸。

Longing for the Red Army

As farmers look forward to a bumper harvest of crop,
Day and night longing for the Red Army the poor never stop.
To destroy despotic landlords and bullies they come here,
Settling old scores and righting the wrongs we bear.

红军来了花不败

罗河川，是花海，
朵朵红花惹人爱，
红军不来花不开，
红军来了花不败。

Flowers are never faded and gone

Luohechuan is like a sea of flowers,
Each bloom is in its brilliant beauty.
No flowers will be found, however,
Ere the Red Army soldiers are here;
Yet they keep fresh and fair forever
When the Red Army soldiers appear.

咱们的红军到南梁

一杆杆红旗一杆杆枪，
刘志丹的队伍到南梁。

长枪短枪红缨子枪，
咱们的红军势力壮。

满天的乌云风吹散，
红军来了晴了天。

打倒了土豪分牛羊，
分了那个田地又分粮。

千年的枯树还了阳，
受苦人翻身喜洋洋。

山丹丹花开红当当，
红军跟的是共产党。

The Red Army is come to Nanliang

Red banner upon red banner, gun upon gun,
Liu Zhidan's army is come to Nanliang.

Red-tasselled spears and guns, short and long,
Our Red Army is developing with power so strong.

The high wind clears off dark storm clouds,
The Red Army's coming sweeps the sky clean.

Local tyrants destroyed, cattle and sheep allotted,
Farm fields and food grains are also distributed.

The dead trees of a thousand years come alive,
The poor people who are now free enjoy a happy life.

Wild lilies burst into blossoms red as flame,
'Tis the Communist Party the Red Army follows.

共产党红军天心顺，
天下穷人都随红军。

赤卫军[①]来旋风队[②]，
掂上个钢枪就打游击。

婆娘女子脚放开，
长头发剪成了短髦盖[③]。

男当红军女宣传，
革命的势力大无边。

---

① 赤卫军是1927—1937年在革命根据地建立的群众武装组织。

② 旋风队是刘志丹、谢子长等在红军和游击队中组建的少年先锋队，作战非常勇猛。“旋风队”是当时群众对“先锋队”的误称，亦含有赞扬的意思。

③ 陇东方言，此处指齐耳短发。

The Party and the Army enjoy popular support,
The poor across China strive to join the Red Army.

The Red Guards[①] and the Whirlwind Teams[②],
Take up guns of steel and join in the guerrillas.

Women and girls their feet no more bind,
And their long hair cut in a bob behind.

Red Army soldiers are men, loudspeakers are women.
Our revolution is developing with power overwhelming.

---

① The Red Guards refer to the armed units of the masses in the revolutionary base areas founded between 1927 and 1937.

② The Whirlwind Teams refer to Young Pioneers founded in the Red Army and the guerrillas by Liu Zhidan and Xie Zichang. They were well-known for being brave and resourceful in battle. "Young Pioneers" were nicknamed "Whirlwind Teams" by the masses in praise of their valor and vigor.

红军起首月明塬[1]

一九三一年，
红军起首月明塬。
谢浩儒[2]，刘志丹，
领导人民把身翻。
打开仓，把粮放，
车子推，口袋掂，
家家户户吃白面。
常开会，常宣传，
打碎旧天换新天。

① 月明塬，正宁县境内一个黄土残塬。
② 谢浩儒，即谢子长，字子长，号浩儒。

The Red Army first rose in revolt in Yuemingyuan[1]

In 1931 it was, when the Red Army
First rose in revolt in Yuemingyuan.
Both Xie Haoru[2] and Liu Zhidan,
To make a revolution the people guided.
Garners were opened, grains divided,
Carried home in sacks or in handcarts,
And thus enough food for all the families.
Publicity activities initiated, meetings held,
For the new they called us to smash the old.

① Yuemingyuan is a loess tableland in Zhengning County.
② Xie Haoru is Xie Zichang, styled Zichang with Haoru as his literary name.

救出千万受苦人

红军红军大救星，
恩情更比父母深；
奋勇打开华池城，
救出千万受苦人。

Saving suffering millions

Great saviors are the Red Army soldiers,
Whose love for us is deeper than parents'.
Bravely have they liberated the Huachi city,
And saved ten thousands of fellow sufferers.

红军来了穷人笑

腊月梅花遍地开，
白军跑了红军来，
红军来了穷人笑，
翻身挺腰站起来。

The poor greeted the Red Army with all smiles

When mume blooms braving the cold winter far and near,
The White Army men have fled afar ere the Red come here.
With the Red Army the poor burst into joyous laughter,
'Cause they will be liberated to stand up straighter.

百姓红军一家人

石榴花儿心里红，
红军爱咱老百姓，
百姓红军一家人，
打倒豪绅享太平。

The people and the Red Army are one family

Our hearts are as red as pomegranate flowers,
The Red Army soldiers love the commoners.
The people and the Red Army are one family,
Down with local tyrants for peace and prosperity.

找红军

受压迫，仇满胸，
受剥削，一世穷，
血债总要血来还，
要想翻身当红军。

背上炒面上南梁，
翻山越岭找红军，
不怕山高沟又深，
跟上红军打敌人。

Seeking the Red Army

Oppressed, full of hatred,
Exploited, lifelong poverty,
Eye for eye, blood for blood,
To rise up you join the Red Army.

With parched flour we're going to Nanliang,
Over hill and dale to look for the Red Army.
Unafraid of mountains high or gullies deep,
We follow the Red Army to fight the enemy.

红旗谣

红旗展，红旗红，
红旗下面是红军，
红军本是受苦人，
受苦人儿要翻身。

红旗飘，红旗绕，
红军力量真不小，
土豪劣绅都打倒，
民团跑了赃官逃。

红旗飞，红旗扬，
分了田地分牛羊，
分了窑洞又分粮，
老百姓来喜洋洋。

红旗来，红旗去，
咱们南梁立苏区，

Ballad of the red banner

Red flags are flapping high in the skies,
Beneath them are the Red Army soldiers.
The soldiers are none other than victims,
Who have set their minds to rise in arms.

Red banners are flying high above the land,
The Red Army has been growing so grand.
Local tyrants and bullies are all overthrown,
Flee corrupt officials, with civil corps down.

Red banners are flying high in the skies,
We've distributed land, goats and cows,
Food grains along with dwelling caves,
And thus the people wear smiling faces.

Red flags fluttering above in the air,
Nanliang has become the Soviet area,

穷人当家做了主，
不受压迫不受欺。

红旗鲜，红旗明，
打起红旗闹革命，
天下穷人随红军，
红旗一展满天红。

红旗好，红旗好，
红旗举起高又高，
跟上红军朝前走，
工农政权牢又牢。

Where we are the masters of our own nation,
Free from oppression and exploitation.

Red banners are streaming far and nigh,
And do fly flaming from sky to sky.
Holding aloft red flags we rise in revolution,
All the poor join the Red Army in succession.

Red banners, bright so bright,
And they do rise high so high.
Let's follow the Red Army to move forward,
The workers' and peasants' power be secured.

红旗插上寨子湾

千里雷声万里闪，
上来些红军闹共产。

共了安边共横山①，
南梁川里扎营盘。

红旗插上寨子湾②，
刘志丹名声传得远。

红军打仗真勇敢，
白军见了吓破胆。

打土豪来分田地，
咱们穷汉把身翻。

跟上咱们的刘志丹，
为咱穷汉打江山。

---

① 安边、横山是地名，均在陕北。

② 寨子湾是南梁政府旧址所在地，在今华池县林镇乡。

Red banners are waving above Zhaiziwan

Thunder rolls loud, lightening flashes far and near,
The Red Army soldiers rising in revolt come here.

Liberating Anbian after Hengshan[①],
They're stationed at Nanliangchuan.

Red flags are flapping above Zhaiziwan[②],
Liu Zhidan's reputation spreads far away.

The Red Army soldiers so fearlessly fight,
The White soldiers are near dead with fright.

Overthrowing landlords and allocating land,
We poor people win liberation and up stand.

Let's follow close behind our Liu Zhidan,
And fight for the poor to free the land.

---

① Anbian and Hengshan are located in Northern Shaanxi.

② Zhaiziwan is the old site for the Nanliang government in Linzhen Township now of Huachi County.

红军常在咱心上

杨柳长在河边上，
松柏长在高山上，
鲜花开在崖畔上，
红军常在咱心上。

The Red Army soldiers stay in our hearts

Poplars and willows grow on river banks,
Pines and cypresses stand on high hills,
Fresh flowers flourish on steep slopes,
Red Army soldiers stay long in our souls.

一杆红旗空中飘

一杆红旗空中飘，
二十五军[①]上来了。

一对对喇叭一对对号，
一面面红旗空中飘。

长枪短枪马拐枪，
一枪枪打死那些连排长[②]。

山丹丹开花红当当，
二十六军[③]驻咱庄。

---

① 二十五军，即程子华、吴焕先、徐海东率领从鄂豫皖根据地长征北上的红二十五军。吴焕先在泾川战斗中牺牲后，即由徐海东、程子华率领，于1935年8月30日至9月8日途径陇东的镇原、庆阳、合水、华池等地，抵达陕北延川县永坪镇，与刘志丹率领的红二十六军、红二十七军汇合，改编为红十五军。

② 连排长，指围追堵截红二十五军长征北上的国民党连排长。

③ 二十六军，即刘志丹等创建和率领的红二十六军。

A red flag is flying on high

A red flag is fluttering high in the air,
The Twenty-fifth Army① is come here.

Trumpet upon trumpet, and horn upon horn,
Bright banners are fluttering high in the sky.

Armed with rifles, pistols and carbines, the Red Army soldiers
Shoot dead those company commanders and platoon leaders②.

Morningstar lilies are in full bloom brilliant red,
At our village the Twenty-sixth Army③ is quartered.

---

① The 25th Army was one branch of the Red Army led by Cheng Zihua, Wu Huanxian and Xu Haidong, making the Long March northwards from the Hubei-Henan-Anhui revolutionary bases. Cheng Zihua and Xu Haidong succeeded Wu Huanxian as heads of the Army after Wu martyred in the battle of Jingchuan. From August 30 to September 8, 1935, it passed by such counties as Zhenyuan, Qingyang, Heshui and Huachi in Longdong and reached Yongping Town of Yanchuan County in Northern Shaanxi, joining the 26th and 27th Armies commanded by Liu Zhidan. And all of them were reorganized as the 15th Army Group.

② Company commanders and platoon leaders refer to those Kuomintang military leaders who had pursued and intercepted the 25th Army in the Long March.

③ The 26th Army was founded and commanded by Liu Zhidan.

搭上云梯上城墙，
格嘣嘣提了一棚枪。

风刮树叶呛浪浪响，
红军哥哥掂上钢枪。

They set up ladder on ladder to climb up the city wall,
And capture the enemy's guns once and for all.

In the rushing wind showers of leaves ruffle the ear,
Guns on the shoulders of the Red Army soldiers dear.

中央红军到陕甘

一道道水来一道道山，
咱们中央红军到陕甘。

一杆杆红旗空中飘，
领兵的元帅是朱毛。

一人一马一杆杆枪，
咱们的红军势力壮。

千里的雷声万里闪，
革命的势力大无边。

The Central Red Army is come to Shaan-Gan

Stream after stream, mountain after mountain,
The central Red Army is come to Shaan-Gan.

Flying above in the air are the red banners,
Zhu and Mao[①] are the military commanders.

One war-horse, one rifle for each soldier,
Our Red Army grows bigger and stronger.

Thunder rolls loud, lightening flashes all over the land,
The revolutionary forces have been growing so grand.

① Zhu and Mao refer to Zhu De and Mao Zedong.

红旗一展天下都红遍

一杆红旗半空中飘，
领兵的元帅是朱毛。

一人一马一杆枪，
咱们的红军势力壮。

工农红军闹革命，
遍地穷人都响应。

革命的势力大无边，
红旗一展天下都红遍。

A red flying flag makes all around it red

A red banner is streaming high in the sky,
The marshals of the army are Zhu and Mao.

Each soldier with a horse and a gun,
The Red Army has power so strong.

The Workers' and Peasants' Red Army make the revolution,
And the poor from far and near rise in revolt with resolution.

The revolutionary forces have grown so grand,
And the red flying flags shine on the whole land.

当兵要当我红军

当兵要当我红军，
处处工农齐欢迎，
官长士兵都一样，
没有人来压迫人。
咿儿呀吱哟，
咿儿呀吱哟，
官长士兵都一样，
没有人来压迫人。

当兵要当我红军，
处处工农齐欢迎，
打倒土豪分田地，
咱们穷人得翻身。
咿儿呀吱哟，
咿儿呀吱哟，
打倒土豪分田地，
咱们穷人得翻身。

Be sure to join the Red Army

Be sure to join the Red Army,
For it's welcomed near and far.
Officers and soldiers are equal to each other,
And no oppression of one on another.
Yi-er-ya-zi-yo,
Yi-er-ya-zi-yo,
Officers and soldiers are equal to each other,
And no oppression of one on another.

Be sure to join the Red Army,
For it's welcomed near and far.
Local tyrants destroyed, land allocated,
We poor people have been liberated.
Yi-er-ya-zi-yo,
Yi-er-ya-zi-yo,
Local tyrants destroyed, land allocated,
We poor people have been liberated.

一杯酒

一杯酒来一盏灯，
捧在门口迎亲人。
红军来到咱陇东，
从此有了好光景。

A wine cup

With a wine cup and a lamp in hand,
Greeting soldiers at the gate we stand.
When the Red Army is here come,
Bright and sunny our days become.

心挨心

山上芦草根连根，
哥闹革命参了军。

你当红军为人民，
妹打游击斗豪绅。

虽然未做同床人，
两颗红心心挨心。

Heart to heart

The roots of reeds on hills entwine each other,
For the revolution my love becomes a soldier.

You go to the Red Army for the people in our country,
I fight as a guerilla to destroy the despotic gentry.

Though we've shared the same bed never,
Our two red hearts beat as one forever.

红旗一展天下都红遍

下面河边牛喝水，
沟里出来些游击队。

大红公鸡窗台上卧，
红军进村好红火。

鸡不叫来狗不咬，
婆姨娃娃都围上了。

今天盼来明天盼，
红军来了盼晴了天。

山丹丹开花红满山，
红军来了革命大发展。

又做饭来又烧茶，
咱们的救星就是他。

一人一马一杆枪，
咱们的红军势力壮。

Blazing far and near when a red flag flies

Down below by the riverside we see an ox drinking,
And some guerilla soldiers out of the valley walking.

On the windowsill a big red rooster is sitting proud,
With the Red Army soldiers the village is loud.

Dogs bark not, nor do cocks crow,
Around the soldiers women and children swarm.

Day and night we yearn for our soldiers dear,
Of clouds the Red Army's coming sweeps the sky clear.

With morningstar lilies blooming, the mountain's all over red,
With the Red Army coming, far and wide our revolution spread.

For them we either make tea or cook meals,
'Cause they are none other than our saviors.

One war-horse, one rifle for each soldier,
Our Red Army grows bigger and stronger.

工农红军来革命，
遍地穷人都响应。

镰刀斧头老镢头，
砍开大路穷人走。

革命势力大无边，
红旗一展天下都红遍。

The Workers' and Peasants' Red Army make the revolution,
The poor from far and near rise in revolt with resolution.

With sickle, hatchet and hoe as arms,
We fight a way out for the poor folks.

The revolutionary force has been growing so grand
That flies a red flag and bright firing the whole land.

咱们军民一家人

望北斗，盼红军，
红旗插到庆阳城。
狗不咬，鸡不叫，
咱们红军进了村。
大娘炕头补军装，
红军担水装满缸。
军爱民来民拥军，
咱们军民一家人。

Army and people are family

Looking up at the North Star, we yearn for Red soldiers,
High above the city of Qingyang are flying red banners.
When the fighters enter the village,
Dogs bark not, nor do cocks crow.
An old dame is sewing uniforms on the edge of Kang[①],
While the Red Army soldiers are filling jars with water.
The Army loves the people, the people support the Army,
The Army and the people unite as one to fight the enemy.

① Kang is a heatable brick bed in Longdong rural areas.

我们是红军的武装

同志们，赶快起来拿刀枪，
我们是红军的武装，
打倒日本强盗和汉奸，
打倒日本建立新中国。
敌人来到了，
我们向前攻，
我们是无敌的红军。
噼哩叭，噼哩叭，
端起枪，向前杀，
打倒日本鬼，
除掉卖国贼。
嗨！我们要求民主解放！

We are the forces of the Red Army

Dear comrades, take up swords and spears,

For we are the forces of the Red Army.

Down with the Japanese robbers and traitors,

Down with Japan; build a new China.

When the foes attack,

We'll beat them back,

For fearless Red Army fighters we are.

Pi-li-pa, pi-li-pa,

Take up guns and charge forward,

Wipe out the Japanese aggressors,

And finish off all the evil traitors.

Hey! For democracy and liberation we strive!

第四章

Chapter Four

抗日之歌

Songs of Resistance Against Japan

我们的天地

天是我们的天，
地是我们的地。
我们的天地，
不能让给日本国。
我们是老百姓，
我们也是兵，
要保卫祖国和家乡，
只有赶走日本军。
打败侵略者，
人民才有好幸福。

Our heaven and earth

Heaven is ours,
And earth is also ours.
Both our heaven and earth
Shouldn't be trampled by Japan.
We are commoners,
And we are also soldiers,
Only by driving the Japanese army off the land,
Can we defend our homestead and motherland.
Only by defeating the Japanese aggressors,
Can the people live in endless happiness.

上前线

敌人进攻边区了，
边区青年们，
坚决动员起来，
参加自卫军。
有枪你赶快背起枪，
大家一起干，
参加军事训练，
准备上前线。
中国人民四万万，
不可降日本。
团结起来有力量，
打垮侵略军。

Starting for the front

The border region is under attack,
Dear young men,
Let's get fully mobilized,
And join in self-defense corps.
Let's go together,
Hasten to take up arms,
Have military trainings,
And get ready for the fight.
All the Chinese people
Shall never surrender to Japan.
So long as we are united closely,
We can crush the Japanese invaders surely.

送 兵

村前村后锣鼓声，
大路上挤满众乡亲，
高头大马哥哥骑，
哥哥光荣去参军，
伊儿呀子哟，
哥哥参军打日本。

Seeing my dearest off to the front

With resounding drumbeat the village is loud,
And the road is thronged with a dense crowd.
Sitting astride a steed, my beloved feels proud,
Honorably he's going to join the army,
Yi-er-ya-zi-yo,
To fight against the Japanese invaders, our enemy.

玩花灯

这是一盏什么灯？
这是一盏救星灯，
什么叫个救星灯？
毛主席，大救星，
领导穷人翻了身。

这是一盏什么灯？
这是一盏太阳灯。
什么叫个太阳灯？
共产党，像太阳，
照亮咱们陕甘宁。

这是一盏什么灯？
这是一盏英雄灯。
什么叫个英雄灯？
大生产，当英雄，
劳动英雄真光荣。

Watching lantern shows

What lantern is it?
A savior lantern it is.
Why is it so called?
Chairman Mao, a big savior,
Leads us to a new life.

What lantern is it?
A sun lantern it is.
Why is it so called?
The Communist Party, like the red sun,
Shines the Shaan-Gan-Ning bright.

What lantern is it?
A hero lantern it is.
Why is it so called?
High praise of heroes in production,
And great glory to labor models.

这是一盏什么灯？
这是一盏王八灯，
什么叫个王八灯？
顽固派，小日本，
勾结起来害百姓。

这是一盏什么灯？
这是一盏拥军灯。
什么叫个拥军灯？
军爱民，民拥军，
军队人民一条心。

这是一盏什么灯？
这是一盏民兵灯。
什么叫个民兵灯？
八路军，自卫军，
组织起来打日本。

What lantern is it?

A turtle lantern it is.

Why is it so called?

Diehards, Japanese devils,

Together against the folks.

What lantern is it?

An army-support lantern it is.

Why is it so called?

Army loves people, people support army,

The army and the people are united as one.

What lantern is it?

A militia lantern it is.

Why is it so called?

The Eighth Route Army and self-defense corps,

Draw together to fight against the evil Japs.

新三恨歌

一恨小日本，
它进攻咱中国，
先把东北吞，
“九一八”炮声响，
侵占了我东三省。
侵占了东三省，
东北的同胞实呀实苦情，
实是苦情，
满胸亡国恨。

二恨汪精卫，
汉奸卖国贼，
南京当傀儡，
认日本作干大[1]，
一心要卖我中华。
人民不依他呀，

① 陇东方言，干爹、义父的意思。

A new song of three hates

First we do hate Japan,
For its invasion of our China,
And occupation of northeast provinces.
On September 18, 1931 it was, when
Japan invaded our northeast China.
During its invasion and occupation,
The people there live in utter misery.
Alas! They really live in utter misery,
Our bosoms swell with rage and hatred.

Next we do hate Wang Jingwei,
The biggest collaborator and traitor,
And a Japanese puppet.
He treats the invaders as his father,
To whom he sells our China.
His treason we are dead against, however;

全国的同胞快呀快起来，
快呀起来，
铲除卖国贼。

三恨孔祥熙，
他的二小姐，
结婚在美国，
赔（陪）嫁妆够几师，
吃饭又穿衣。
这都是咱血汗，
把这些洋奴才喂呀喂的肥，
思量起呀，
实叫人生气。

All the countrymen, let's pull together as ever,
And jump into action immediately,
To weed out this traitor completely.

Then we do hate Kong Xiangxi,
For his second daughter
Got married in America,
Whose dowries, so substantial,
Would suffice thousands of soldiers.
We are none but the men
Who feed and fatten them all.
When we think of this,
Our hearts are filled with burning flames of fury.

劝当兵

头一杯茶呀，
劝我的大[1]呀，
儿去当兵你在家呀，
儿去当兵打日本。

二一杯茶呀，
劝我的妈呀，
儿去当兵你不要怕呀，
打败日本转回家。

三一杯茶呀，
劝我的妻呀，
我去当兵你莫哭啼呀，
家里家外要靠你。

---

① 陇东方言，意思是父亲。

To be a soldier

The first cup of tea
Is for my father:
You stay home when I'm off to be a soldier,
To be a soldier that fights the Japanese invader.

The second cup of tea
Is for my mother:
Worry not about me when I'm off to be a soldier,
I won't come home until beating the Japanese invader.

The third cup of tea
Is for my wife:
Weep and wail not when I'm off to be a soldier,
On you everything depends, home related or not.

四一杯茶呀，

劝我的妹呀，

哥去当兵你跟着嫂嫂睡呀，

老人娃娃笑哈哈。

The fourth cup of tea
Is for my younger sister:
Be with your sister-in-law when I'm off to be a soldier,
Both the old and the young burst into tinkling laughter.

做针线

做针线，
做针线，
针线做得真颇烦[1]，
想起小日本呀，
要灭咱中原[2]。

大炮轰隆隆，
飞机在空中，
占了武汉和广东。
边区真危险呀，
大难在眼前。

大难在眼前，
赶紧做针线，

① 陇东方言，不耐烦的意思。
② 中原，这里指代中国。

Doing needlework

Doing needlework,
Doing needlework,
Of needlework I'm sick,
Of evil Japan so I think,
Who's invading our China.

Cannons are roaring,
Planes in heaven hovering,
Wuhan and Guangdong are fallen.
In deadly danger is our homestead,
The national disaster looms ahead.

Alas! The evil days have come,
Let's hasten to do needlework,

做双军鞋亲人穿。

打垮小日本呀，

保卫咱家园。

And make shoes for dear soldiers.

Only by defeating the evil invaders,

Can our homeland be well guarded.

拥军歌

正月里来是新春，
家家户户来拥军。
赶上猪羊出了门，
送给那英勇的八路军。
咳哟咳哟咳哟，
送给那英勇的八路军。

八路军自家的人，
它和咱们一条心。
坚持抗战有功劳，
赫赫大名天下闻。
咳哟咳哟咳哟，
赫赫大名天下闻。

天下闻名的总司令，
一心爱咱们老百姓，
为咱们日子过得美，

Song of supporting the army

The first moon welcomes the Spring Festival,
To the Army each family gives support possible.
We drive the pigs and goats out of the fold,
And send them to the soldiers bold.
Hai-yo-hai-yo-hai-yo,
And send them to the soldiers bold.

The ERA soldiers and people are family,
Their hearts and ours beat as one firmly.
They drive the Japanese invaders off the land,
And earn the great fame that rings thro' the world.
Hai-yo-hai-yo-hai-yo,
And earn the great fame that rings thro' the world.

Zhu De, a world-famed commander and kind,
Loves the commoners with heart and mind,
For us poor people to live a life good,

发动了生产大运动。
咳哟咳哟咳哟，
发动了生产大运动。

八路军呀个个能，
保卫咱边区陕甘宁。
帮咱割来又帮咱种，
哪一个百姓不领情。
咳哟咳哟咳哟，
哪一个百姓不领情。

你领情来我领情，
赶上猪羊快快行。
一心爱戴总司令，
一心那拥护八路军。
咳哟咳哟咳哟，
一心那拥护八路军。

He wages the great production campaigns.
Hai-yo-hai-yo-hai-yo,
He wages the great production campaigns.

The ERA soldiers, one and all, are very capable,
Who defend the Border Region from aggression,
And help us with farm work as much as possible,
Each and every civilian shows his appreciation.
Hai-yo-hai-yo-hai-yo,
Each and every civilian shows his appreciation.

None feels not gratitude to dear soldiers deep,
Let's send them the pigs and sheep we keep.
We love our Commander Zhu heart and soul,
We support the Eighth Route Army heart and soul.
Hai-yo-hai-yo-hai-yo,
We support the Eighth Route Army heart and soul.

飞针走线做鞋忙

十月里来天气凉，
飞针走线做鞋忙，
莲叶帮子梅花底，
亲人穿上打东洋。

Busy with shoe sewing

The weather is cold when the tenth lunar month comes,
The needles fly when we keep busy with sewing shoes.
Lotus leaves broidered on uppers, mume blooms on soles,
For dear soldiers to wear to strike the Japanese aggressors.

人民救星人民爱

千条线，万根针，
绣块金匾送恩人。
人民救星人民爱，
救星就是毛泽东。

The people's beloved savior

With thousands of threads and needles,
We are embroidering a golden plaque,
For the people's savior of Mao Zedong,
Who's dearly beloved by his fellowmen.

八路军真正好

八路军，真正好，
坚持抗战有功劳，
不怕流血不怕苦，
奋勇杀敌把国保。

八路军，打仗好，
打得鬼子没命跑，
敌后开辟根据地，
收复地方真不少。

八路军，纪律好，
事事办得都公道，
不打人来不骂人，
处处和平打交道。

八路军，爱民好，
对咱百姓真关照，

To the Eighth Route Army our praise shall be

The Eighth Route Army soldiers are so bold,
And perform meritorious deeds and untold.
They know no hardship, fear no bloodshed,
And kill the foes bravely the state to defend.

The Eighth Route Army soldiers fight heroically,
And make the evil enemies rush around frantically.
They set up base areas behind the enemy lines,
And take back hills and rills lost on the front lines.

The Eighth Route Army, well-disciplined,
Everything they do fair and square,
Anybody they neither blame nor beat,
And everybody as a friend they treat.

The soldiers' love of people never stops,
For us they take pains to do good deeds:

帮咱耕来帮咱种，
帮咱送粪又锄草。

八路军，搞生产，
开荒种地大凤川，
自种粮食自纺织，
为咱百姓减负担。

八路军，是救星，
一心为咱老百姓，
为了百姓享安宁，
英勇牺牲真光荣。

八路军，子弟兵，
它和人民心连心，
人民拥护八路军，
军民团结向前进。

Ploughing the land, planting crops,
Delivering manure and hoeing up weeds.

The soldiers engage in farm production,
And bring the wasteland into cultivation.
Grow crop and weave cloth for themselves
So as to lighten the burden of us civilians.

The Eighth Route Army soldiers, our saviors,
Shed blood and sweat for the commoners.
They would rather make supreme sacrifice
For all the fellow men to have a life nice.

The Eighth Route Army is the people's army,
The Army and the people are linked heart to heart.
The people's army the people love and support,
The Army and the people unite to march forward.

做军鞋

“七七”卢沟桥，
日本兵变了，
杀人又抢财，
还把那房屋烧。

上海炸得焦，
南京危险了，
国难已当头，
谁愿做亡国奴。

前线抗日军，
冰天雪地中，
为祖国为民族，
英勇杀敌人。

一没布鞋穿，
二没草鞋蹬，
衣裳破袜子烂，
有谁给他缝。

Sewing shoes for soldiers

On July 7, 1937 at Lugou Bridge,
Japan waged a war against China.
Burning and killing fill the land,
Raping and looting are hard to stand.

Shanghai has been bombed out,
Nanjing's in a desperate situation.
China has met the day of danger,
But never be a conquered nation!

The soldiers on the front,
Braving the winter snows,
For the country and people
Fearlessly fight the foes.

No shoes do they have,
Nor sandals do they wear.
Worn are clothes, torn socks,
Who would make the mends?

妹妹年纪小，
妈妈眼睛麻，
小嫂嫂在灯下，
急忙把鞋纳。

打开针线包，
鞋面没有了，
剩下的日本货，
剪铰[①]用火烧。

向爹要鞋面，
向妈要针线，
要给那子弟兵，
做双布鞋穿。

家里没有钱，
叫我好作难，
拆东墙补西墙，
先要顾前线。

嫁衣裁鞋面，
耳坠换针线，

① 陇东方言，剪的意思。

My sister is too young,
While mother too old,
Only sister-in-law is stitching soles
In the faint flickering lamp light.

The sewing parcel I unfold,
Yet nothing for vamp it hold
But the Japanese stuff
That I cut into pieces and burn up.

Ask father for shoe vamp, and
Ask mother for thread and needle,
To make new pairs of cloth shoes
For our beloved soldiers in battle.

There's no money at home I find,
That really puts me in a big bind.
Then, robbing Peter to pay Paul,
The only way that arises in my mind.

From my own bridal array I cut the insteps,
For needle and thread I sell my earrings.

怎么裁怎么缝，
大小我摸不准。

照爹鞋样铰，
爹爹脚面高，
害怕那战士们，
穿上不合窍①。

一更月照东，
点上清油灯，
纺车吱吱响，
绳绳拧得匀。

二更月渐高，
妹妹已睡着了，
关了门闭了窗，
添油把灯挑。

手戴上铜顶针，
急忙把鞋缝，
鞋底上纳钉钉，

① 陇东方言，不合适的意思。

But neither do I know how to tailor or sew,
Nor am I sure about what is the right size.

Making shoes in father's size,
Yet my father has arch high.
So I'm afraid that the shoes
May not fit the soldiers.

When the moon shines low in the east bright,
A vegetable-oil lamp up I light.
With the creak-creak of my spinning wheel,
The thread I spun proves fine and even.

When the moon in the sky climbs higher,
My younger sister is in a heavy slumber.
The door I close and the window I shut,
Replenish the lamp with oil, trim the wick.

A thimble on my finger putting,
I hurry on with shoe sewing,
On soles stitching sturdy knots,

鞋帮上扎匀匀。

三更月当空，
夜静更又深，
猫儿陪伴我，
摇尾念着经。

鞋底已扎成，
鞋帮也扎成，
头儿有点昏，
手儿也有些疼。

四更月偏西，
两眼睡意重，
想起了子弟兵，
一时提精神。

眼睛揉一揉，
头发揪一揪，
绳绳抿一抿，
鞋儿要做成。

And on uppers making small stitches.

When the moon hangs overhead right,
Late and quiet is the very night.
For company I only have a cat,
It waves its tail with purring slight.

Soles have been finished,
And uppers also done.
Yet I feel a bit faint,
And my hands hurt.

When the moon sinks low in the western skies,
So heavy with sleepiness are my eyes.
When thinking of the soldiers, however,
I stop being drowsy forever.

Rubbing my eyes,
Pulling my tresses,
And moistening the thread on my lips,
As a new day dawns I must finish my shoes.

五更鸡儿鸣，
一夜没停针，
鞋儿做成了，
再写上信一封。

家中都安宁，
地方也太平，
雨水多庄稼好，
亲人们莫牵心。

英雄的子弟兵，
听我说一声，
穿上这双鞋，
奋勇杀敌人。

We work all night without a break.
When the cock crows at daybreak,
We've finished new pairs of shoes,
And also a letter about family affairs.

Peace and pleasure in all the families,
And safe and sound is our homestead,
Good weather promises good crops ahead,
Dear ones, no more worries rest your head.

Dear brave soldiers and bold,
A word needs to be told—
Put on these pairs of shoes,
To fight fearlessly the foes.

四季歌

春天里，春风吹，
漫山遍野镢头挥。
夏天里，庄稼长，
抗日军民锄草忙。
秋天里，糜子黄，
欢天喜地去打场。
冬天里，雪花飘，
练兵整训本领高。

Song of four seasons

In spring the vernal wind blows,
All over the hill slopes people wave hoes.
Summer sees crops growing,
Soldiers and civilians busy with weed clearing.
In autumn millet turns golden day by day,
To do the threshing people are happy and gay.
Winter sees snowflakes swirling and dancing,
Troops trained to raise the capacity of fighting.

十杯酒

一杯子酒儿一点红，
敬给救星毛泽东，
你是天上红太阳，
照得边区红彤彤。

二杯子酒儿双手敬，
敬给咱们总司令，
抗日杀敌领大兵，
劳苦功高老英雄。

三杯子酒儿放明光，
敬给靠山共产党，
你是人民的指路灯，
照到哪里哪里亮。

四杯子酒儿清又清，
敬给亲人八路军，

A toast song

Here's the first cup of wine, a red heart,
We toast Mao Zedong, our dear savior.
You, like the red sun high up in the sky,
Shine bright the border region far and nigh.

Here's the second cup of wine, with two hands,
We toast Zhu De, our dear commander.
You lead a mighty army to beat the Japanese invader,
And a hero of great fame worthy of the name.

The third cup of wine sparkles bright,
We toast the Communist Party, our dear support.
The beacon to the people you are,
And bring light wherever you go.

The fourth cup of wine looks crystal clear,
We toast the Eighth Route Army, our soldiers dear.

流血流汗为百姓，
斟杯酒儿谢恩情。

五杯子酒儿甜又甜，
敬给县长和专员，
领导群众闹生产，
丰衣足食有吃穿。

六杯子酒儿味儿浓，
敬给劳动英雄们，
领头互助闹变工，
为了大家常操心。

七杯子酒儿美味香，
敬给抗属表心肠，
你们的亲人上前方，
大家代耕理应当。

八杯子酒儿味儿美，
敬给咱们的好姊妹，
纺线织布勤生产，
千辛万苦多劳累。

九杯子酒儿酒味醇，
敬给民兵自卫军，

You have shed blood and sweat for the poor folks,
We offer a toast to you to show our heartfelt thanks.

Here's the fifth cup of wine sweet so sweet,
We toast the magistrates and commissioners.
In the production front rank you always stand,
People are well fed and clad on the borderland.

The sixth cup of wine has strong flavor,
We toast our great heroes of labor.
In labor exchange and mutual aid you take the lead ever,
And worry about the people and production forever.

The seventh cup of wine smells sweet,
We toast families of the soldiers at the front.
Your kinsmen are fighting for our land,
We ought to lend you a helping hand.

The eighth cup of wine smells delicious,
We toast our dear and diligent siblings.
Spinning, weaving and farming all the way,
You toil and moil all your day.

The ninth cup of wine tastes mellow,
We toast militiamen and self-defense corps,

防特除奸打顽军，
千家万户享太平。

十杯子酒儿斟满盅，
敬给边区好弟兄，
咱们大家一条心，
抗战定能早成功。

Against enemy agents, traitors and stubborn armies
That brings peace and pleasure to millions of families.

The tenth cup is overflowing with wine,
We toast our good brothers from the borderland.
So long as all the people join heart and hand,
We can surely drive the invaders off the land.

留守兵团军歌[1]

我们是人民的手臂，
人民是我们的心脏，
爱护土地，
爱护人民，
参加生产，
减轻他们的负担。
没有他们，
我们就不能生存。
我们是革命的队伍，
为人民争取解放，
谁来进攻谁就灭亡。
大炮骏马培养我们，
我们喜欢书本和枪。
我们巡逻，

① 这首歌在抗日战争时期曾在八路军后方留守兵团所辖的陇东驻军三八五旅部队中广泛传唱。

The military song of the left-behind regiment[1]

We are the people's arms,
And the people our hearts.
Love the land,
Love the people,
And join farm production
To help ease their burden.
Without them,
We could not survive.
We are the revolutionary army
To win liberation for the people,
And destroy those who attack us.
Canons and horses cultivate us,
Who love both books and guns.
We are patrolling,

---

① This song was widely circulated among the 385th Brigade soldiers who were then stationed in Longdong under the control of the left-behind regiment of the Eighth Route Army during the Anti-Japanese War.

我们守望，

在中国西北广阔的高原上。

敌人进攻，

我们就瞄准射击。

我们是光荣的队伍，

为国家守卫边疆，

谁来进攻谁就灭亡！

We are watching
On the vast northwest plateau of China.
When the enemies attack,
In no time we'll beat them back.
We are a glorious army
For the country to defend the borderland,
And destroy those who attack our motherland.

生产谣（节选）

春　耕

春天里来地开冻，
上山开荒大变工，
咱们大家一条心，
黄土变成金。

四月里来麦苗青，
多种糜谷有收成，
前方后方齐心干，
准备大反攻。

驮　盐

庄稼青草长满山，
草锄过了走三边[1]，
吆着毛驴去驮盐，
赚下钱来闹生产。

① 陇东民间对陕北定边、安边和靖边的简称。

Ballad of production (Excerpt)

Spring ploughing

When spring comes round, thaws the ground,
For reclamation of hillsides folks are bound.
If all the people are of one mind,
The yellow earth can become gold.

In April wheat seedlings are a green lush,
More millet in fields promises a crop rich.
Both the front and the rear together stick,
And get ready for a general counterattack.

Trading salt

Crops and green grass all over the mountains,
After weeding the fields we go to the frontiers①.
Our donkeys are loaded with sacks of salt,
The money earned will be used in production.

---

① The frontiers refer to Dingbian, Anbian and Jingbian in northern Shaanxi in Longdong.

秋　收

秋天里来好时光，
满山糜谷黄又黄，
割得快呀打得忙，
丰衣足食喜洋洋。

冬　藏

一年四季忙得欢，
男耕女织齐生产，
粮食堆成山呀，
不怕遭困难呀，
今年好收成呀，
有吃又有穿呀，
军队百姓齐心干，
打走鬼子好过太平年。

Harvesting in autumn

Autumn is a good season for harvest,
Hillsides are golden with ripe millet.
Reaping and threshing, no one is idle,
Well fed and clad, everyone is glad.

Storing in winter

Everybody keeps busy all the year round,
Men are furrowing and women weaving.
The grain we reap are piled high as hill,
And thus fear not crop failures we will.
This year there has been a harvest good,
We dread not shortage of clothing and food.
The army and the people hand in hand join,
Drive the foes off and a peaceful year enjoy.

自卫军[1]

照亮了，看清了，
看清的是什么事情？
就是咱边区的自卫军。
咱们自卫军把武器，
锈的磨它个明的，
烂的打它个新的，
老[2]的磨它个快的，
短的安它个长的。
把他特务顽固分子，
比作个老鼠，
咱们边区没有一个窟窿，
满墙根里跑，
它就是不得进去。

---

① 自卫军是抗日战争时期边区一种民兵性质的革命武装组织。
② 陇东方言，钝的意思。

Self-defense corps[①]

Brightly it shines, clearly we see,

And what is it that clearly we see?

'Tis self-defense corps in our border region!

They keep their weapons in good condition:

Polishing them bright if rusty,

Forging them anew if broken,

Sharpening them again if blunt,

And adding length to them if short.

A spy is presumed

To be a mouse;

All the border region men unite so closely

That it makes furtive attempt all the way,

No hole made to steal through anyway.

① It is a kind of militia organization in the border region during the Anti-Japanese War period.

大凤川

大凤川，大凤川，
往日荒凉无人烟。
今日三八五旅到，
一年叫你换容颜。
虎狼要绝迹，
丛林要斩断，
野草烧光开良田，
要叫凤凰飞上天。
大凤川要变万凤川，
千秋万代美名传。

Dafengchuan

O Dafengchuan, my dear Dafengchuan,
Of old you were ever bleak and desolate;
But now the 385th Brigade is stationed here,
Who will change your face in a single year.
Grass and grove cleared away,
Wolves and tigers driven away.
We shall open up the wilds in any way,
And score a victory in the fight to reclaim the wasteland.
Dafengchuan is sure to have rich rice-producing farmland,
And will live by fame won by creating more arable land.

抗日军政大学[1]校歌

黄河之滨，
集合着一群，
中华民族优秀的子孙；
人类解放，
救国的责任，
全靠我们自己来担承。
同学们，努力学习，
团结、紧张、严肃、活泼，
我们的作风。

---

① 抗日军政大学，全名为“中国人民抗日军事政治大学”，简称“抗大”，是在抗日战争时期由中国共产党创办的培养军事和政治干部的学校。其前身是“中国人民抗日红军大学”，1936 年 12 月，校部由保安迁至延安，并于 1937 年初改为此名。从 1938 年底到 1945 年春，抗日军政大学先后在陕甘宁、华北、华中等革命根据地建立了 14 所分校。

Song of Anti-Japanese Military and Political College of China①

By the shores of the Yellow River
Gather together a galaxy
Of fine youth from the Chinese nation;
Nobody but us have to bear the burden
Of human liberation
And national salvation.
Comrades, study hard,
And stick to our motto:
Being united, alert, earnest and lively.

① Anti-Japanese Military and Political College of China, also known as Kangda, was a school established by the Communist Party of China for cultivating and training military and political cadres during the War of resistance against the Japanese invaders. It grew out of the Chinese People's Anti-Japanese Red Army School which was moved from Bao'an to Yan'an in December 1936, and renamed in January 1937. From the end of 1938 to the spring of 1945 the College opened as many as 14 branch schools in such revolutionary base areas as Shaan-Gan-Ning, North China, Central China, etc.

同学们！积极工作，

艰苦奋斗，英勇牺牲，

我们的传统。

像黄河之水，

汹涌澎湃，

把日寇驱逐于国土之东。

向着新社会，

前进！前进！

我们是劳动者的先锋！

Comrades, work hard,

And carry on our fine red tradition:

Plain living, arduous struggle and noble sacrifice.

Like the rushing waters

Of the Yellow River,

We shall drive the Japanese devils off this land.

Toward a new society,

Forward! Ever forward!

Pioneer laborers we are!

春天歌

冰河在春天里解冻，
万物在春天里复生，
全世界被压迫的妇女，
在“三八”喊出了自由的吼声。
山坡上，镢头抖着歌声在挥舞，
火一样的热情，烧在我们身上；
火一样的力量，放在我们工作上。
身似铁，志如钢，困难障碍一扫光。

Song of spring

All the frozen rivers start to melt in spring,
All the things on earth come to life in spring.
All the oppressed females in the world
Shout the cry of freedom on Women's Day.
All the hoes on the hillside swing up and down
To the tune of the laborers' song.
Ardor like fire, all ablaze in our breast,
Vigor like fire, all aglow in our work.
With body as strong as steel, and resolve as hard as iron,
We sweep clean obstacles and difficulties, however great.

抗大七分校[①]校歌

建军的骨干，

革命的青年，

在豹子川扎下大营盘。

赶上葫芦河，

学习南泥湾，

① 1943 年，抗大七分校进驻陇东根据地的合水县城关、华池县豹子川等地。1944 年 3 月，抗大七分校的校部在校长彭绍辉率领下由合水迁驻华池县东华池古城。全校三个大队，5200 余人。一大队九个分队驻大凤川，二大队九个分队仍驻豹子川，三大队八个分队驻平定川，女生队两个分队驻东华池。在三年多时间里，学员们边学习、边生产，共挖窑洞 690 多孔，箍石窑 30 多孔，建新房 40 余间，盖起可容纳 2000 多人的大礼堂，开垦荒地 6 万多亩。1944 年全校生产粮食 8600 多石，养猪 1300 余头，羊 1100 多只，牛 100 多头。1947 年 7 月，抗大七分校撤离华池时，移交华池县人民政府余粮 7000 多石。这首校歌中的“葫芦河”，原驻有陕甘宁晋绥联防军骑兵旅，后又驻新四旅，均因开荒生产业绩显著而闻名陇东根据地乃至陕甘宁边区。

Song of the Seventh Branch School of Kangda[1]

The pillars of the army,

The youth of the revolution,

Are all stationed in Baozichuan.

Catch up with Huluhe,

And learn from Nanniwan as a model,

---

① In 1943 the Seventh Branch School of Kangda was moved to Chengguan of Heshui County, and Baozichuan of Huachi County, respectively. In March 1944, it was moved to Donghuachi of Huachi County. The branch school consisted of three brigades with more than 5,200 people. The first brigade included 9 teams who were stationed in Dafengchuan; the second brigade also involved 9 teams who lived in Baozichuan; the third brigade covered 8 teams who dwelled in Pingdingchuan, with two female teams living in Donghuachi. For more than three years, the students in Kangda were engaged in study as well as in production. They dug roughly 690 dwelling caves, built more than 30 caves out of stones, constructed 40 new houses, and an auditorium which could hold around 2,000 people. In addition, they reclaimed more than 60,000 *mu* of wasteland. In 1944 the branch school yielded over 8,600 *dan* of food grain, raised over 1,300 pigs, 1,100 sheep and 100 head of cattle. In July 1947 when the seventh branch school was withdrawn from Huachi County, it offered over 7,000 *dan* of grain food to the People's Government of Huachi County. Huluhe mentioned in this song was where the cavalry brigade of the Shaan-Gan-Ning-Jin-Sui Joint Defense Forces and later the New Fourth Brigade were once encamped. They were renowned in Longdong Base and Shaan-Gan-Ning Border Region for both their reclamation and good production performances.

把荒山变成理想的乐园。

学文又学武，

打仗又生产，

毛主席指引我们向前。

向前！向前！

我们永远向前！

努力学习，

刻苦锻炼，

学好本领，

奔赴斗争最前线。

Into a real haven we'll turn a barren hill.

Receive knowledge and have military drill,

Fight in war and engage in production still,

Chairman Mao shows us the way forward.

Forward! Ever forward!

We'll forever march on forward!

Comrades, study hard,

Train hard,

Learn military skills,

And go out to battle.

春天百花歌

春天百花放，
日本鬼子进攻我们的边疆，
西北的老百姓武装上战场，
要保卫父母兄弟姐妹儿郎。

西北人民一起来干，
陕甘宁地方好作游击战，
打得敌人进退两难，
要他活活死在我们面前。

When the spring breaks into flowers

When the spring breaks into flowers,
The Japs began to attack our frontiers.
The armed northwest people rise in revolution
To ward dear families from foreign aggression.

The northwest people join heart and hand
To fight guerrilla wars on the borderland,
Of which the enemies find no way out,
And they'll be doomed to be wiped out.

纺线线

棉花车车滴溜溜转，
好像朵朵白玉莲。
白生生的棉花纺成了线，
送到咱们的工厂，
织布做衣衫。
军队穿，百姓穿，
人人穿上人人暖。
自力更生，
战胜困难，
抗大学生，
劳动锻炼，
学好本领，
开赴抗日的最前线。

Spinning threads

Spinning wheels of cotton are whirling and whirling
Like clusters of the white lotus flowers blooming.
White cotton is spun into threads
Brought to our manufactory,
Where we weave the cloth to clothe
Both soldiers and civilians,
Warming one and all.
Students in Kangda,
Be self-dependent,
Overcome difficulties,
Make us tough in labor,
And master military skills
To go to the War against the Japanese aggression.

开荒曲

鸡叫三遍天发白，
劳动的队伍上山来，
东方的太阳放光彩，
这一片荒地我们开。
哎哟嗨，哨子一声响，
哎哟嗨，镢头举起来，
樱桃好吃树难栽，
小米饭好吃荒难开。

Ballad of reclamation

When cocks crow a third time, bright is the sky,
The laboring people stream up the hills high.
The sun in the east throws down its golden beam,
Here's a vast area of the wasteland we'll reclaim.
Ai-yo-hai, when the whistle for operation blows,
Ai-yo-hai, we set to work, waving high our hoes.
Hard to grow cherries though they are good to eat,
Hard to clear land to plant millet though it is sweet.

缴公粮

新谷子，黄又黄，
新糜子，香又香，
收毕[1]了庄稼，
大家喜洋洋，
今年[2]要多缴些救国公粮。

黄米粒，金灿灿，
小米子，味美香，
车推毛驴驮，
翻沟过山梁，
九万石[3]公粮赶快送前方。

---

① 陇东方言，庄稼收割结束的意思。
② 今年，指 1941 年。
③ 九万石，指 1941 年新宁县征缴公粮的任务。

Delivery of tax grain

Fresh grains, yellow so yellow,
Fresh millet, sweet so sweet.
When the harvest's done,
The gloom people are feeling is gone,
This year[①] we're supposed to pay more grain tax to the state.

Yellow grains glint like gold,
Fresh millet smells so sweet.
Loaded by donkeys or in handcarts,
Over hills and dales,
We deliver all the tax grain without delay to the front.

---

① Here it refers to the year of 1941.

第五章

Chapter Five

边区之歌
Songs of the Border Region

边区就是咱的家

天上有颗北斗星，
中国有个毛泽东，
他的办法多又好，
条条为咱老百姓。

石榴树上开红花，
边区就是咱的家，
谁敢动它一星土，
咱拿性命保卫它。

The border region is our home

Up in the sky there is the Big Dipper,
Down in China there is a Mao Zedong,
Who works out many good measures,
In which each and every one pleasures.

Red flowers on pomegranate trees bloom,
And the border region is our home.
If a single inch of our land is to be invaded,
We'll even risk our lives to defend it.

毛主席像太阳

毛主席，像太阳，
我们边区像一盆花，
他照得我们大家，
兴兴旺旺是一家。

Chairman Mao is like the red sun

Chairman Mao's like the sun in heavens,
And our border region, a pot of flowers.
He spreads his beams on all of us bright,
Who live a life of happiness and delight.

我们边区像清泉

我们边区就好像一道清泉，
用是用不干的，
越用越多。
我们粮草积得多，
我们边区就兵强马壮，
尽打胜仗。
打仗回来是丰衣足食，
换上他三套新衣裳；
鸡猪牛羊肉，
还有大白馍，
吃起来真香。

我们大家组织起来，
种地的人，
做工的人，
做生意的人，

Our border region is like a clear spring

Our border region is like a clear spring,
With an inexhaustible store of water sweet,
The more you draw, the more it springs up.
We stock up on food and fodder so sufficient
That we have soldiers strong and horses sturdy,
And also many victories in battle.
With ample food and clothing,
We change into new clothes when back from fighting;
And eat chicken, pork, beef and mutton,
As well as big bread made of wheat flour,
What tasty food we have!

Now let's join hand and heart!
Farmers,
Workers,
And businessmen,

三人合一心，

黄土就变成金。

加上难民，

四人合一心，

力大就几千斤。

我们老百姓，

和我们边区的政府一条心，

这就是五人合一心，

力量就几万斤。

我们八路军在前方打仗，

我们五人给他用力量。

If ever these three are one,
Then the yellow earth can yield grain of gold.
With refugees included,
There're four whose hearts beat as one,
Then we have strength weighing thousands of *jins*.
If we civilians are united
With the border region government,
There're five with one heart and one mind,
Then we have strength as great as tens of thousands of *jins*.
The Eighth Route Army men fight on the front without fear,
There're five people who are behind them in the rear.

我们边区团结得像铁桶

我们边区，
团结得像铁桶，
那些像老鼠一样的，
汉奸和特务分子，
找不到一个窟窿。

Closely united are our border region men

Our border region men
Unite closely as a metal bucket.
Those traitors and spies,
Who act like mice,
Fail to find a hole to squeeze through.

文教大会歌

学文化，有办法，
你教我来我教他；
讲卫生来办医药，
读报识字唱秧歌。

Song of education

By teaching and helping each other,
We begin to make ourselves literate;
Turn to hygiene, set up medical units,
Go thro' newspapers, sing with Yangko.

自己动手建学校

胜利了，我们胜利了，
豹子川现在繁荣了，
课堂一座又一座，
窑洞一排又一排，
肥猪满圈哼哼哼，
群群牛羊满山跑。
我们的课堂盖得好，
我们的窑洞建得牢，
门窗桌椅和用具，
样样都是自己造，
克服了困难不怕苦，
自己动手建学校。

We build schools ourselves

Victory, O victory, victory comes!

Baozichuan has become prosperous:

Row on row of classrooms,

Row on row of dwelling caves;

Pigs fat and round snort and snuffle in the sties,

Herds and flocks roam about over the slopes.

Solid and secure are classrooms,

Strong and sturdy dwelling caves.

Doors, windows, desks, chairs and teaching appliances

Are all made by ourselves.

Surmount difficulties and fear not hardships,

We work hand in hand to build our schools.

放脚歌

妇女姊妹们，
快呀快放脚，
缠脚多不好，
走起路，
咯咯拧拧摇摇摆，
你看多难过！
妇女姊妹们呀，
快呀快放脚。

Song of unbinding the feet

Women and girls, our dear sisters,
Quickly, quickly unbind your feet,
For bound feet bring you no good
But harm: while walking
You keep swaying and shaking,
How you walk, you do know!
Women and girls, our dear sisters, so,
Quickly, quickly unbind your feet.

绣荷包

一绣共产党，
心胸如海洋，
容量宽大政策好，
人人都热爱。

二绣毛主席，
他是人民的灯，
照得边区放光明，
花开遍地红。

三绣劳动者，
你们真光荣，
民先报解放报，
都有你们名。

四绣边区民，
人民真热心，

Making an embroidered pouch

The first embroidery is the Communist Party,
Who has a mind broad as boundless seas,
And makes more preferential policies,
Which each and every man cherishes.

The second embroidery is Chairman Mao,
Who serves the people as a beacon light,
And shines over the border region bright,
Blossoms bloom red far and wide.

The third embroidery is the laborers,
You are such respectable workers,
On *Minxian* and *Jiefang* newspapers
Appear your glorious names.

The fourth embroidery is the borderers,
You are really concerned about the fighters.

驴驮马载人也挑，

都是慰劳品。

The items loaded by donkeys, horses and persons

Are all gifts given to our dear heroic soldiers.

边区好

咱们边区好地方，
山高水绿好风光。
粮食足，兵马强，
五谷丰登好年景。
政府号召大生产，
耕一余二多增产。
开荒地来纺线线，
不愁吃来不愁穿。
过新年，真喜欢，
红灯笼，挂门前。
男女都把新衣换，
秧歌社火闹得欢。
边区生活真美好，
领导全靠共产党。

The border region is a nice place

A good and nice place is our dear borderland,
For here rills green glide, hills high stand.
Strong are soldiers, sturdy horses, sufficient food,
And also a golden harvest promises a year good.
By launching the large-scale production campaign,
To a greater height we have raised the crop yields.
By spinning threads and reclaiming the wilds,
Sorrow attends not us who are well fed and clad.
New Year people happily and merrily celebrate,
Red lanterns hang over each household's gate.
Men and women are in new clothes arrayed,
Yangko and Shehuo are joyfully played.
Under the leadership of the Communist Party,
People in border area are leading a life of plenty.

选举歌

满坬稻秫哪一苯高？

人里头挑人数谁好？

思量又思量，

比较又比较，

把那好人的名字，

写上了选举票。

Song of election

Of all the sorghums on the mountain slope,
Which grows the tallest?
Of all the people I have ever known,
Who is to be elected the fittest?
Think it over and over,
Compare them again and again,
I write the name of the one I choose
Down on my ballot ticket.

玩花灯

提起了正月正呀，
人人喜盈盈，
大街市上玩花灯，
人马闹哄哄。

人人喜盈盈呀，
今年大不同，
家家户户挂红灯，
红灯照得明。

红灯照得明呀，
穷人翻了身，
共产党来了救穷人，
咱们翻了身。

毛主席是救星呀，
照亮了咱们的心，

Parading lighted lanterns

In the first month of the lunar year,
All people are beaming with cheer,
Parading lighted lanterns everywhere,
Shouts and neighs echoing here and there.

Everybody is happy and merry,
For this year tells a different story.
Each house hangs lanterns red,
Whose light is brightly spread.

Each and every house is illuminated,
For all the poor have been liberated.
'Tis none but the Communist Party
Who assists us to live a life of plenty.

Chairman Mao is a big lodestar,
Who beams bright in everybody's heart.

边区人民一条心，

黄土变成金。

If the borderers with one mind work hard,

Even the yellow earth can become gold.

穷人翻身乐哈哈

枯树逢春开了花，
穷人翻身乐哈哈。
鞭儿吆着黄牛走呀，
种出自己的好庄稼。

The liberated poor beam with smiles

As the withered tree in spring breaks into flowers,
The poor who are liberated burst into broad smiles.
With a whip I drive my oxen to plough the land,
Where I grow and reap good crops with my hand.

太阳出来照地红

太阳出来照地红，
“红区”有个毛泽东。
他爱百姓像亲人，
领导着“红区”百姓大翻身，
他是百姓大救星。

桃花开花红艳艳，
“红区”地方好乐园。
政府县长百姓选，
人人有权提意见。
丰衣足食光景好，
牛羊牲口养满圈。
受苦人只要勤劳动，
当英雄来中状元。

The rising sun shines the earth red

The rising sun shines red the earth here,
Mao Zedong lives in the Red area.
Like his kinsmen the people he loves,
As the big benefactor he serves,
And steers people to liberation.

Peach blossoms bloom red and fair,
The Red area proves a paradise rare,
Where we ourselves elect government officials,
Where we're free to voice views on public affairs.
Well fed and well clothed, we lead a life better,
And the cattle and sheep in number are greater.
So long as the poor are industrious and laborious,
They'll do great deeds and win victories glorious.

闹变工

正月里来正月正，
毛主席号召闹变工，
你帮我来我帮他呀，
大家才能都翻身。

二月里来刮春风，
出牛送粪把地耕，
你出牛来我出力呀，
咱们大家一条心。

三月里来是清明，
组织变工快下种，
精耕细作多上粪呀，
秋后才有好收成。

四月里来四月八，
动员大家种棉花，

Labor exchange

'Tis in the first month by the lunar calendar,
Chairman Mao calls on us to exchange labor.
Only if we offer aid and help to one another,
Can all of us live a life of leisure and pleasure.

In the second month the vernal wind is blowing,
Time it is for manure delivery and land ploughing.
Come and give, you your cattle and I my labor,
For farm work let's pool our resources together.

The third month meets the Qingming Festival,
Time it is for seed-sowing through aid mutual.
With careful cultivation and enough manure,
We're to reap a good harvest in autumn sure.

In the fourth month, on the eighth day,
Mobilize people to grow cotton with delight,

今年棉花好收成呀，
纺线织布做鞋袜。

五月里来天气长，
人人上山去开荒，
增加耕地益处多呀，
政府奖励不征粮。

六月里来麦子黄，
变工收割人人忙，
打下麦子推成面呀，
送给咱军队做干粮。

七月里来七月七，
合格套牛耕麦地，
咱们大家齐心干呀，
当了英雄去开会。

八月里来秋风凉，
谷子糜子满山黄，
快收快打快快藏呀，
防奸反特要加强。

For whose harvest of this year is now in sight;
For of which cloths and clothes are made alway.

Days are growing long when lunar May is at hand,
Everybody opens up the wasteland on the hillside.
More benefits come with increasing arable land,
On which no grain levies are imposed far and wide.

The sixth month makes wheat golden hour by hour,
Everybody's busy with the harvest day after day.
The grains we reap will be ground into flour,
And sent to the army soldiers for food all the way.

In the seventh month, on the seventh day,
To drive our sturdy oxen afield we're gay.
Let's shoulder our arms all together,
And vie to be first with one another.

In the eighth month the cool autumn winds rise,
Ripened grain turns golden all over the hillsides.
Reap apace, thresh apace, and store apace, apace,
Efforts made to guard against traitors and spies.

九月里来九重阳，
大家开会缴公粮，
家家都要实来报呀，
抗日救国理应当。

十月里来天气冷，
纺线织布要加劲，
穿上棉衣去训练呀，
保卫咱们陕甘宁。

十一月来天气寒，
组织起来去驮盐，
运输工作做得好呀，
赚下钱来闹生产。

腊月里来整一年，
大家拥军要争先，
人人都把礼物送呀，
军民一心走向前。

The ninth month brings the Double Ninth Festival,
Meetings are held calling for tax grain as much as possible;
About its harvest every family's required to be honest,
'Tis our bounden duty to pay grain taxes to the state soonest.

In the tenth month when it turns cold,
Speed up yarns and cloths production,
Then we'll have military training in warm coat,
And guard our border region from aggression.

In the eleventh month when it grows bitter,
People go to trade salt with good organization.
We'll try our utmost to do the business better,
And make money enough to boost production.

The twelfth month reports the end of a whole year,
To the army we're supposed to offer our support strong.
Each and every one should give gifts to soldiers dear,
The Army and people will march on together for long.

军民大生产[①]

解放区呀么嗬嗨，
大生产呀么嗬嗨，
军队和人民，
西里里里嚓啦啦啦嗦罗罗罗呔，
齐动员那么嗬嗨！

开梢林呀么嗬嗨，
开荒地呀么嗬嗨，
边区的男男女女，
西里里里嚓啦啦啦嗦罗罗罗呔，
爬满山那么嗬嗨！

自力更生么嗬嗨，
丰衣足食么嗬嗨，

---

① 这首陇东民歌的歌词，为音乐舞蹈史诗《东方红》导演团依据人民艺术家张寒晖的《边区十唱》原词整理改编。《东方红》舞台艺术电影片拍竣于1965年10月1日。标题为《陇东红色歌谣》收辑者所加。

The great production of the Army and the people[1]

In the liberated areas,
The great production is in full swing.
The army and the people
Are all mobilized and motivated.

Chop trees and bushes down,
To open up the wasteland.
Borderers, male and female,
Are crowding up the slopes.

Self-dependence assures us
Of ample food and clothing,

① The lyrics of this Longdong folk song were adapted and modified by a group of directors from *Singing of the Border Region* by the well-known artist Zhang Hanhui for a music and dance epic named *Red in the East*, whose film was finished on National Day in 1965. The title was given by the collector of *Longdong Red Songs*.

加紧生产，

西里里里嚓啦啦啦嗦罗罗罗呔，

为抗战那么嗬嗨！

又能武呀么嗬嗨，

又能文呀么嗬嗨，

要问我什么队伍，

一、二、三、四！

八路军那么嗬嗨！

Speed up production
For the War against the Japanese aggression.

I am able to wield well
Both the pen and the sword.
When asked which army I am in,
One, two, three, four!
I am in the Eighth Route Army!

军民大生产[①]

解放区呀么嗬嗨，
大生产呀么嗬嗨，
军队和人民，
西里里里嚓啦啦啦嗦罗罗罗呔，
齐动员呀么嗬嗨。

变工队呀么嗬嗨，
互助组呀么嗬嗨，
劳动的歌声，
西里里里嚓啦啦啦嗦罗罗罗呔，
满山川呀么嗬嗨。

妇女们呀么嗬嗨，
都争先呀么嗬嗨，

① 这首陇东民歌的歌词，是陕西省文艺工作者于 1971 年依据人民艺术家张寒晖的《边区十唱》原词整理改编，且定名为《军民大生产》，为 1972 年中央人民广播电台播出的“陕甘宁边区五首革命民歌”之一。

The great production of the Army and the people[①]

In the liberated areas,
The great production is in full swing.
The army and the people
Are all mobilized and motivated.

Labor-exchange teams
And mutual-aid groups;
Songs of the laborers
Thrill over the hill slopes.

Women and girls
Strive to be heroes or models;

---

① The lyrics of this Longdong folk song were adapted by some Shaanxi performing arts professionals according to *Singing of the Border Region* by a famous artist named Zhang Hanhui, and the song was officially named *The Great Production of the Army and the People*. It was one of the five revolutionary songs of the Shaan-Gan-Ning Border Region broadcasted by the Central People's Broadcasting Station in 1972.

手摇着纺车，
吱咛咛咛吱咛咛咛嗡嗡嗡嗡吱儿，
纺线线呀么嗬嗨。

自己动手么嗬嗨，
丰衣足食么嗬嗨，
加紧生产，
西里里里嚓啦啦啦嗦罗罗呔，
为抗战呀么嗬嗨。

又能武呀么嗬嗨，
又能文呀么嗬嗨，
人问我什么队伍，
一、二、三、四！
八路军呀么嗬嗨。

Turn their spinning wheels,
Creak-creak and whirr-whirr,
To spin threads.

Self-dependence assures us
Of ample food and clothing;
Speed up production
For the War against the Japanese aggression.

I am able to wield well
Both the pen and the sword.
When asked which army I am in,
One, two, three, four!
I am in the Eighth Route Army!

军民大生产[①]

解放区呀么嗬嗨，
大生产呀么嗬嗨，
军队和人民，
西里里里嚓啦啦啦嗦罗罗罗太，
齐动员那么嗬嗨！

开梢林呀么嗬嗨，
开荒地呀么嗬嗨，
边区的男男女女，
西里里里嚓啦啦啦嗦罗罗罗太，
加油干那么嗬嗨！

妇女们呀么嗬嗨，
都争先呀么嗬嗨，

① 这首陇东民歌的歌词，综合了音乐舞蹈史诗《东方红》导演团、陕西文艺工作者分别整理的歌词，更趋完美，成为《军民大生产》的定型歌词。张寒晖为这首民歌的词作者。

The great production of the Army and the people[①]

In the liberated areas,
The great production is in full swing.
The army and the people
Are all mobilized and motivated.

Chop down trees and bushes
To open up the wasteland.
Borderers, male and female,
Work with added vigour.

Women and girls
Strive to be heroes or models;

① The lyrics of this Longdong folk song were compiled and modified from the words of two songs with the same title by the group of directors for a music and dance epic *Red in the East* and some Shaanxi performing arts professionals respectively. The lyrics of this version tend to be perfect and became the final version for this song, officially with Zhang Hanhui as its lyricist.

手摇着纺车，
吱咛咛咛吱咛咛咛嗡嗡嗡嗡吱，
纺线线那么嗬嗨！

自力更生么嗬嗨，
丰衣足食么嗬嗨，
加紧生产，
西里里里嚓啦啦啦嗦罗罗呔，
为抗战那么嗬嗨！

又能武呀么嗬嗨，
又能文呀么嗬嗨，
人问我什么队伍，
一、二、三、四！
八路军那么嗬嗨！

Turn their spinning wheels,
Creak-creak and whirr-whirr,
To spin threads.

Self-dependence assures us
Of ample food and clothing;
Speed up production
For the War against the Japanese aggression.

I am able to wield well
Both the pen and the sword.
When asked which army I am in,
One, two, three, four!
I am in the Eighth Route Army!

十绣金匾[①]

正月里闹元宵，
金匾绣开了，
金匾绣咱毛主席，
领导的主意高。
一绣毛主席，
人民的好福气，
你一心爱我们，
我们拥护你。

① 这首长达10小节80行的陇东优秀民歌《十绣金匾》是20世纪40年代初由陕甘宁边区新正县（今庆阳正宁县）一位名叫汪庭有的木匠编唱的，描绘了一幅边区党政军民同心同德、各项建设事业欣欣向荣的美好图景。《十绣金匾》在其广泛传唱的过程中，不断得到人民群众和专业文艺工作者的再创造，歌词也随之做了重大改动，原作的“十绣”被精炼为“三绣”，更名为《绣金匾》。在解放战争时期充分发挥了战斗作用，成为广泛传唱、妇孺皆知、人人喜爱的优秀民歌。

The golden banner with ten embroideries[①]

The Lantern Festival meets January lunar,
We begin embroidering the golden banner.
It starts with Chairman Mao's portrait,
A leader with ambition and foresight.
The first embroidery is Chairman Mao,
What a good leader the people have!
You work for us ever,
We support you forever.

① The lyrics of this fine Longdong folk song consist of ten stanzas with 80 lines. They were created in the early 40s of the 20th century by a carpenter named Wang Tingyou living in Xinzheng County (now Zhengning County of Qingyang). This song depicts the wonderful scenes in which the Party, government, army and people work together to build the border region. When widely sung among the masses, the song experienced recreation and revision from both the people and the professional artists with the lyrics adapted and shortened from ten embroideries to three embroideries and with the title modified into *Embroidering the Golden Banner*. In the War of liberation it played a significant role in fighting and became a fine folk song with great popularity.

二月里刮春风，
金匾绣的红，
金匾绣的是，
边区陕甘宁。
二绣陕甘宁，
世事多太平，
军和民大团结，
大家一条心。

三月里是清明，
金匾绣三层，
金匾上绣的是，
模范八路军。
三绣八路军，
抗战下决心，
对民众多恩情，
爱国爱人民。

四月里立夏天，
金匾绣的宽，
金匾上绣的是，
八路军生产。

The spring breeze blows in February lunar,
Skillfully embroidered is the golden banner,
Whereon is stitched none other than
The Shaan-Gan-Ning Border Region.
The second embroidery, the Border Region,
Where all is peace and delight;
Where army and people join their hands,
And as one beat all their hearts.

The Tomb-sweeping Day falls in March lunar,
Delicately embroidered is the golden banner,
Whereon is stitched none other than,
A model Eighth Route Army man.
The third embroidery, the brave Eighth Route Army,
Who battle against the Japanese invaders, our enemy,
And show much care and concern for the masses,
More than self the country and people they cherish.

Lunar April welcomes the season of summer,
Nicely embroidered is the golden banner,
On which is stitched none other than
The Eighth Route Army engaged in production.

四绣军生产，
比民忙大半，
夜晚守警戒，
白天务庄田。

五月里五端阳，
金匾绣的亮，
金匾上绣的是，
边区老百姓。
五绣老百姓，
抗战最热情，
组织起自卫军，
打倒小日本。

六月里热气腾，
金匾绣花云，
金匾上绣的是，
民众的劳动。
六绣民劳动，
有利有名声，
行行出状元，
二流子成英雄。

The fourth embroidery, the soldiers in production,
They are busier by far than we civilians,
'Cause in the night sentry they have to stand,
Yet in the daytime they work out in the field.

Lunar May brings the Dragon Boat Festival,
Brilliantly embroidered is the golden banner,
Whereon is stitched none other than
The commoners in the border region.
The fifth embroidery is the commoners,
With great zeal who battle the invaders;
They themselves organize self-defense corps,
And fight fearlessly against the invading Japs.

Lunar June is the hottest month in summer,
Beautifully embroidered is the golden banner,
Whereon is stitched none other than
The civilians who are busy at work.
The sixth embroidery is the laborers,
Labor brings them fame and fortune.
Every trade has its master,
Even a loafer makes a hero.

七月里七月半，
金匾绣金线，
金匾上绣的是，
妇女闹生产。
七绣女生产，
织布又纺线，
加入识字组，
要当女状元。

八月里八月半，
金匾绣的圆，
金匾上绣的是，
边区合家欢。
八绣好家常，
卫生身体强，
全家人都和气，
民主好商量。

九月里九重阳，
金匾绣的长，
金匾上绣的是，
移民上天堂。

A month hotter is July Lunar,
Fine is the golden banner,
Whereon is stitched none other than,
The women joining farm work.
The seventh embroidery is industrious women,
Who spin threads and weave cloth,
And learn to read by joining study groups,
For they strive to be female model workers.

Autumn comes in August lunar,
Splendid is the golden banner,
Whereon is stitched none other than
Harmony and happiness in borderland families.
The eighth embroidery is their homely joys,
Healthy and hygienic each and every man keeps;
Family members get 'long well with one another,
And family issues settled thro' counsel together.

The Double Ninth Festival in September lunar,
Exquisitely embroidered is the golden banner,
Whereon is stitched none other than
The refugees immigrating to the happy land.

九绣难民来，

政府好优待，

老户们帮助他，

吃用有办法。

冬月里天气寒，

金匾十绣全，

金匾上绣的是，

政府恩情宽。

政府恩情宽，

冬学处处办，

有吃有穿有文化，

快活过新年。

The ninth embroidery is the immigrated refugees,
Who receive favored treatment from the government,
And thoughtful assistance from the local resident,
Both shelter and bread are all secured.

When the autumn days are gone,
The golden banner is done.
The last embroidery is
The government of preferential policies,
Far and near winter schools are operated,
We're well fed and clad, and well-educated,
The happy New Year is merrily celebrated.

绣金匾[①]

正月里闹元宵，
金匾绣开了，
金匾绣咱毛主席，
领导的主意高。

二月里刮春风，
金匾绣的红，
金匾上绣的是，
救星毛泽东。

一绣毛主席，

① 这首陇东民歌的第四段（即二绣总司令）歌词，是陕甘宁边区军民在传唱汪庭有的《十绣金匾》过程中新编的一段歌词；其第五段（即三绣八路军）歌词，是抗日战争胜利后，边区军民针对国民党反动派发动全面内战的严峻形势而编唱的，并将原词中的“边区陕甘宁”改为“救星毛泽东”。同时，为适应战争环境，将汪庭有原词的十段（每段八句）精炼为五段（每段四句），定名为《绣金匾》。

Embroidering the golden banner[1]

The Lantern Festival meets January lunar,
We begin embroidering the golden banner.
It starts with Chairman Mao's portrait,
A leader with ambition and foresight.

The spring breeze blows in February lunar,
Brilliantly embroidered is the golden banner,
Whereon is stitched none other than
Mao Zedong, our big benefactor.

We first embroider Chairman Mao,

① The lyrics of the fourth stanza in this Longdong folk song were revised by the army and the people from the version of *The Golden Banner with Ten Embroideries* by Wang Tingyou, a well-known peasant song writer in Longdong. The lyrics of the fifth stanza were adapted by the borderers to target Kuomintang reactionaries who launched the Second Civil War after the victory of the Anti-Japanese War with "the Border Region Shaan-Gan-Ning" modified into "the savior Mao Zedong". Under the wartime conditions, Wang Tingyou's version of ten stanzas with eight lines each was simplified and shortened into the one of five stanzas with four lines each and renamed as *Embroidering the Golden Banner*.

人民的好福气，
你一心为我们，
我们拥护你。

二绣总司令，
革命的老英雄，
为人民谋生存，
能过好光景。

三绣八路军，
坚决打敌人，
消灭了反动派，
全国享安宁。

What a good leader the people have!
You work for us ever,
We support you forever.

Next we embroider Commander-in-chief Zhu,
A great hero and true in the revolution,
You go to lengths greater
For the people to live a life better.

Then we embroider the Eighth Route Army,
Who fight resolutely against the enemy.
After they've destroyed the reactionary,
Peace broods over the whole country.

绣金匾[1]

正月里闹元宵，
金匾绣开了，
金匾绣咱毛主席，
领导的主意高。

二月里刮春风，
金匾绣的红，
金匾上绣的是，
救星毛泽东。

一绣毛主席，
人民的好福气，
你一心为我们，

① 这首陇东民歌的第五段（即三绣周总理）歌词，是在粉碎“四人帮”后，人民艺术家郭兰英于1977年初将《绣金匾》原词第五段“三绣八路军”改为“三绣周总理”而演唱的，使之成为一首献给人民领袖的颂歌。

Embroidering the golden banner[①]

The Lantern Festival meets January lunar,
We begin embroidering the golden banner.
It starts with Chairman Mao's portrait,
A leader with ambition and foresight.

The spring breeze blows in February lunar,
Nicely embroidered is the golden banner,
Whereon is stitched none other than
Mao Zedong, our big benefactor.

We first embroider Chairman Mao,
What a good leader the people have!
You work for us ever,

---

① The lyrics of the fifth stanza in this Longdong folk song were adapted by Guo Lanying, a famous folk-song singer, in early 1977 from "the third to embroider is the Eighth Route Army" to "the third to embroider is Premier Zhou" after the smashing of the Gang of Four. Thus, this folk rhyme has become a song dedicated to our great leaders.

我们拥护你。

二绣总司令，
革命的老英雄，
为人民谋生存，
能过好光景。

三绣周总理，
人民的好总理，
鞠躬尽瘁为革命，
我们热爱你。

We support you forever.

Next we embroider Commander-in-chief Zhu,
A great hero and true in the revolution,
You go to lengths greater
For the people to live a life better.

Then we embroider our beloved Premier Zhou,
You are the best premier of the people,
We dearly love you, for the revolution
You work with unselfish devotion.

五枝花

（男）什么花开花朝太阳？

什么人拥护共产党？

（女）葵花儿开花朝太阳，

老百姓拥护共产党。

（男）共产党，怎么样？

（女）好像天上的红太阳，

照的边区亮堂堂。

（男）什么花开花身上穿？

什么人话儿记心间？

（女）棉花儿开花身上穿，

毛主席的话儿记心间。

（男）毛主席，说什么？

（女）号召咱们大生产，

边区要变米粮川。

（男）什么花开花大路边？

Five flowers

(M) What flower in full bloom turns towards the sun?
What people support the Communist Party?
(F) The blooming sunflowers turn towards the sun,
The ordinary people support the Communist Party.
(M) How's the Communist Party?
(F) It's like the red sun in the skies,
In its golden radiance the border region lies.

(M) What turns into clothes when blooming well?
Whose words should in our mind dwell?
(F) Cotton turns into clothes when blooming well,
Chairman Mao's words should in our mind dwell.
(M) What does Chairman Mao tell us to do?
(F) He calls on us to speed up production on the land,
The border region will have rich rice-producing farmland.

(M) What flowers are in full bloom by the road side?

什么人坚决来抗战？
（女）马莲花开花大路边，
八路军坚决来抗战。
（男）八路军，怎么样？
（女）个个都是英雄汉，
英勇抗战美名传。

（男）什么花开花耀眼红？
什么人和咱们一家人？
（女）桃花开花耀眼红，
八路军和咱们一家人。
（男）一家人，怎么样？
（女）军民联合一条心，
一心要赶走小日本。

（男）什么花开花迎春天？
什么人迎接胜利年？
（女）迎春花开花迎春天，
同盟国迎接胜利年。

（男）迎接胜利怎么办？
（女）加紧准备大反攻，
抗战胜利在眼前。

Who resolutely fight the Japs far and wide?

(F) Malian flowers are in full bloom by the road side,
The Eighth Route Army fight the Japs far and wide.

(M) How are the Eighth Route Army men?

(F) Each and every one is brave and bold,
Whose brilliant glory fills the world.

(M) What flower blooms blazing red?
Who are family with us civilians?

(F) Peach flowers bloom blazing red,
The Eighth Route Army and the people are family.

(M) How's the family?

(F) The army and the people join heart and hand,
And drive the Japanese invaders off the land.

(M) What flower bursts heralding the approach of spring?
And who are now celebrating the year of victory?

(F) Primroses burst greeting the advent of spring,
The Allies are celebrating the year of victory.

(M) What shall we Chinese people do next?

(F) Hasten to prepare for the general counterattack,
The victory over Japan is close at hand.

毛主席号召大生产

（合）毛主席号召大呀大生产，
咱们个个都喜欢，
伊儿呀子哟，
男女老少，
一齐动员，
都来闹生产。
（男）加油开荒，
（女）加劲纺线，
（合）咱们都来闹生产，
得儿呀哈一个呀哈，
（男）加油开荒，
（女）加劲纺线，
（合）咱们生产做模范。

（合）劳动英雄真呀真光荣，
咱们个个当英雄，
伊儿呀子哟，

Chairman Mao calls on us to promote production

(C) Chairman Mao calls on us to speed up production,
To it each and every one responds with full support.
Yi-er-ya-zi-yo,
Men and women, young and old,
All should
Engage in production.
(M) Speed up opening up the wilds,
(W) Speed up spinning threads,
(C) Let's engage in production.
Yi-er-ya-zi-yo,
(M) Speed up opening up the wilds,
(W) Speed up spinning threads,
(C) Let's strive to be model workers.

(C) Glory, glory to the laborers!
Let's strive to be labor heroes,
Yi-er-ya-zi-yo.

（男）老汉娃娃，
（女）婆娘女子，
（合）都来当英雄。
（男）加紧生产，
支持前线。
（合）齐心打败那小日本，
得儿呀哈一个呀哈，
（女）加劲生产，
有吃有穿，
（合）男女老少喜盈盈。

（合）毛主席号召组织起来，
加劲生产闹竞赛，
伊儿呀子哟，
（女）纺线组，
（男）变工队，
（合）赶紧办起来。
（男）大家动手，
丰衣足食，
（合）咱们边区人人爱，
得儿呀哈一个呀哈，
（女）努力生产，
支援前线，
（合）红花咱们英雄戴。

(M) Young and old,
(W) Women and girls,
(C) All strive to be heroes.
(M) Speed up production,
And support the front.
(C) Let's jointly defeat the evil Japs,
Dei-er-ya-ha-yi-ge-ya-ha.
(W) Speed up production,
We'll be well fed and clothed.
(C) Men and women, young and old, beam with joy.

(C) Chairman Mao calls on us to have organization,
Speed up production and promote labor emulation,
Yi-er-ya-zi-yo.
(W) Thread-spinning groups,
(M) Labor-exchange teams,
(C) Get quickly organized.
(M) Let's work together,
We'll live in abundance.
(C) Our border region each and every one cherishes,
Dei-er-ya-ha-yi-ge-ya-ha.
(W) Speed up production,
And support the front.
(C) Red flowers on the breasts of our heroes.

第六章

Chapter Six

解放之歌

Songs of Liberation

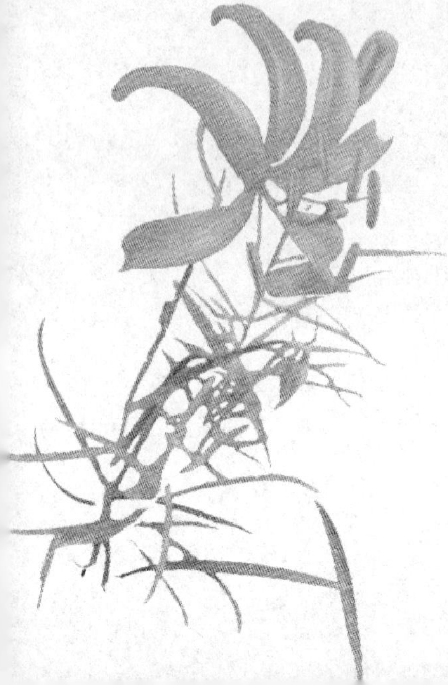

准备打胜仗

正在河边洗衣裳，
听见一声大炮响，
转身回家来呀，
哎哟，回家对娘讲。

回到家里对娘讲，
白军队伍快进庄，
赶快做预防呀，
哎哟，赶快做预防。

哥哥背枪头里走，
弟弟放哨上山冈，
手拿红缨枪呀，
哎哟，放哨上山冈。

嫂嫂忙着烙干粮，
爹爹急忙装军粮，
准备打胜仗，
哎哟，准备打胜仗。

Ready to fight for victory

When washing by riverside, happy and gay,
Suddenly I heard a bang from afar by day.
In no time I went my homeward way,
Ah, I hastened home to inform my Mom.

Back home I dashed to Mom and told her,
Our village the White Army was about to enter;
Let's hurry up and get ready for the fight,
Ah, let's hurry up to be ready for the fight.

Elder brother, gun on back, hurried on ahead,
And younger brother following close behind,
With a red-tasseled spear in his hand,
Ah, he went to the hilltop to guard stand.

My sister-in-law was baking bread for the family,
And father busy with food grain for the Army.
Let's get ready and fight for victory,
Ah, let's get ready to fight for victory.

毛主席领导咱打江山

千里的雷声万里闪，
毛主席领导咱打江山。

山上的松柏山下的花，
共产党领导咱当了家。

青天蓝天蓝格莹莹的天，
共产党来了咱好喜欢。

太阳上来满山山红，
受苦人过上了好光景。

Chairman Mao leads us to fight for a new life

Thunder rolls loud, lightening flashes far and wide,
Chairman Mao leads us to fight for a better world.

High on the hills stand pine and cypress trees, blossoms below,
We're masters of the country when the Communist Party we follow.

The blue sky, the blue sky, the blue and clear sky,
The Communist Party we welcome in spirits high.

Hills and dales are aglow with the rising sun light,
The suffering people have days sunny and bright.

毛主席举旗向前进

青天蓝天蓝英英的天，
这是什么人的队伍上了前线？

一杆杆哟大旗红又红，
上面绣着镰刀斧头五角星。

毛主席举旗向前进，
后面跟着百万兵。

保卫咱的土地和牛羊，
解放军英勇上战场。

解放军老百姓不分离，
永远跟着咱毛主席。

Chairman Mao leads us onward

Blue sky, blue sky, blue and clear sky,
Whose army is going to the frontline?

A big banner is streaming, brilliant and red,
With sickle, hammer and stars embroidered.

A mighty army with firm resolution
Follows Chairman Mao to make the revolution.

To protect our land, sheep and cattle,
The PLA men bravely go to the battle.

The PLA men and the people go apart never,
And closely follow Chairman Mao forever.

送夫参军

正月里正月正，
送丈夫去当兵，
手提上小包袱，
把丈夫送出门。

二月里刮春风，
送丈夫去参军，
为人民去参军，
好好打敌人。

三月里三月三，
叫丈夫好好干，
打垮了蒋介石，
咱夫妻再团圆。

四月里四月八，
叫一声小娃娃，

Sending my loving husband into the army

In January by the lunar calendar,
To the army I send my husband.
With a small parcel in my hand,
Off to the gate I see my dear lad.

Lunar February brings a vernal wind,
To join the army I send my husband.
For the people you go to the army,
With all your powers fight the enemy.

In the third month, on the third day,
I tell my man to fight with all his might.
The day that Chiang Kai-shek is defeated,
We, husband and wife, will reunite.

On the eighth day in April lunar,
My child I order

你写上一封信，
捎给你大大[①]。

五月里五端阳，
家家生产忙，
有什么困难处，
政府来帮忙。

六月里麦上场，
打碾快入仓，
支援咱人民军，
杀敌保家乡。

① 陇东方言，指爹爹或者父亲。

To write a letter
And send it to his father.

Lunar May sees the Dragon Boat Festival,
Every household is engaged in farming;
With care and concern from the government,
Hardships we have been overcoming.

Wheat on the threshing ground Lunar June brings,
Let's hasten to thresh and store wheat grains.
We offer enough food to feed the people's army,
So that they, to guard our state, fight the enemy.

送公粮

翻一架山来过一道梁，
吆上个毛驴驴去送公粮，

送公粮送在了前线上，
支援咱解放军打老蒋，

麦粒儿饱来小米子香，
子弟兵吃饱打胜仗，

解放军杀敌为人民，
咱们送粮表一表心。

Deliver tax grain to the front

We go over hills and through vales all the way,
And drive our donkeys loaded with tax grain.

We deliver tax grain to the battle ground,
So the PLA soldiers make Jiang's men flee around.

Wheat grains are plump and millet grains sweet,
With enough food, the foes our soldiers will defeat.

For the people the PLA soldiers battle against the enemy,
And delivery of tax grain is our way to support the army.

拥军小唱

大雪飞，一片白，
敲锣打鼓举红旗，
男女老少劳军去，
天寒地冻心欢喜。

你牵羊，我捉鸡，
猪肉吊子手里提，
豆腐粉条一大堆，
担挑车推拥军去。

解放军，真英勇，
流血牺牲为咱们，
恩情难忘重如山，
送点东西表心意。

Song of supporting the army

Snowflakes are dancing, the sky and ground all white,
Beating gongs and drums, red flags raised to a height;
Men and women, young and old, go reward the troops,
'Tis cold outside, yet our hearts are aglow with delight.

Sheep, cock, and pieces of pork,
Loads of vermicelli and bean curd,
On shoulder poles or in handcarts,
We carry to our dear brave soldiers.

The People's Liberation Army men are bold,
How many laid their lives for us 'tis untold.
Their kindness to us is heavy as a mountain,
Gift-giving is our way of supporting the army.

解放小调

毛主席呀真英明，
领导人民闹革命，
他是人民的大救星，
哎哟，他是人民大救星。

解放军呀真英勇，
解放中国几十省，
杀的蒋匪乱逃奔，
哎哟，杀的蒋匪乱逃奔。

十月里呀花儿红，
人民首都定北京，
解决中国大事情，
哎哟，解决中国大事情。

A ditty of liberation

Chairman Mao proves great and wise,
Who leads the people in revolt to rise.
He is a big liberator of the people,
Ah, he is a big liberator of the people.

The PLA soldiers fight far and wide,
Driving Jiang's men nowhere to hide.
Many a province they have liberated,
Ah, many a province they have liberated.

In October when flowers blow fair and red,
Beijing is the capital of New China made,
The major national issue is thus settled,
Ah, the major national issue is thus settled.

革命成了功

东方红，太阳升，
中国出了个毛泽东，
革命到如今，
哎哟，革命到如今。

解放军，老百姓，
齐心合力打敌人，
革命成了功，
哎哟，革命成了功。

The revolution ends in victory

Red is the east, comes up the sun,
China's brought forth a Mao Zedong,
Who leads us to make the revolution,
Ah, he leads us to make the revolution.

The PLA soldiers and the civilians,
Stick together to fight the enemies,
So the revolution ends in victory,
Ah, the revolution ends in victory.

牧童歌

早放羊，晚放羊，
从早放到月东上。
自幼失去爹和娘，
牧童两眼泪汪汪。
就是有爹娘，又能怎么样？
五年大水，十年旱，
二十年兵灾失家乡。
早放羊，晚放羊，
春夏秋冬四季忙，
羊儿吃饱了，牧童饿断肠，
主人吃的牛羊肉，
牧童尸骨照月光。

Song of a shepherd boy

Tending sheep in the morn, tending sheep in the eve,
The shepherd boy was herding the flock all day long.
'Cause as a child he had been bereaved of parents,
The boy's eyes were always brimming with tears.
What if he had
Mom and Dad!
Flooding for five years, drought for ten years,
Homeless from wars for twenty more years.
Tending sheep in the morn, tending sheep in the eve,
The shepherd boy was herding the flock all year long.
When the goats he grazed ate their fill,
The shepherd was empty-stomached still.
While enjoying tasty beef and mutton his lord was beaming,
The boy's bones scattered on moon-blanched wilds gleaming.

豹子川大合唱

（一）

这儿有广大的牧场，
牧场上走着成群的牛羊。
你听，那牛背上的牧童，
笛儿吹得多悠扬！
这儿有肥美的土地，
土地生长着糜子和高粱。
你看，那荷锄的农民，
脸上放着喜悦的光。

山高高，遍山绿，
水曲曲，村外绕。
道路伸得远，
窑洞阳光照。
梅鹿山上走，
野鸡咯咯叫。
风吹庄稼绿波动，

A chorus Baozichuan makes

I

Here spreads a wide expanse of grassland,
Whereon herds and flocks are grazing.
Hark! The herd boy on the cow back
Upon his pipe a sweet song is playing!
Here spreads a vast stretch of fertile field,
Whereon millet and sorghum are growing.
Look! The farmer who's shouldering a hoe
Wears a face with delight and radiance glowing.

The high mountains are clad in glistening green,
The winding stream girdles the village with sheen.
As far as our eyes can reach, the roads go,
The dwelling caves bathed in warm sunshine glow,
The spotted deer on the hills are wandering at will,
And the pheasants clucking still.
In the light winds like green waves crops sway,

一阵谷香吹来了。
朝霞升起天刚晓，
雄鸡叫得早，
人们起得早。
遍野山歌歌声高，
豹子川哟，
你这个地方真正好！

（二）

革命起来了，
人民大声笑，
起来了，起来了，
革命起来了。
人民像怒潮，
军阀台子倒。
游击队拿起枪，
少先队拿起刀，
几千年的束缚解放了，
几千年的枷锁打碎了。
嗨，全国人民起来呀，
这儿有的是自由，

And the millet fields are breathing sweet alway.
The morning sun springs up when the day dawns,
The roosters crow early,
And the people rise early.
Over the hills echo songs, loud and long,
Ah! Baozichuan,
What a nice place you are!

II

When the revolution is spreading,
The people roar with laughter.
Revolution, O revolution,
Spreading is the revolution.
Like the surging tides,
The people rush to overthrow warlords.
Guerilla soldiers take up shot-guns,
Young pioneers swords and spears.
Thousands of years of chains are shaken,
Thousands of years of fetters are broken.
Hey! Arise, all the fellow men.
Here everybody enjoys freedom he seeks after,

有的是欢笑。
山上插着红旗，
红旗迎风飘。
我们要把这鲜红的旗帜，
举得更高更高更高。

自从来了刘志丹，
咱们的日子不一般。
打倒了土豪和地主，
推翻了军阀和赃官，
没有地的人民有了土地，
没有穿的有了穿。
自己动手自己享，
没有人再来抽税捐。
这儿的人民相亲相爱，
这儿的人民上了天。

刘志丹，刘志丹，
刘志丹呀是清官，
他和人民在一起，
他和人民骨肉连。
刘志丹，刘志丹，
刘志丹呀是清官，

Here everybody beams with smiles sweeter.
Above on the heights
Red flags do rise.
These gorgeous banners we have to hold
Higher, higher, and still higher.

Since Liu Zhidan is come to Nanliang,
Our life is quite different from bygone days.
Down with tyrants and landlords,
Down with corrupt officials and warlords.
Those without land are given land,
Those in want of clothes are well clad.
To supply ourselves we work with our own hand,
None levy a tax on us any more across the land.
The people here are dear to each other,
The people here live in the happy realm together.

Liu Zhidan, O Liu Zhidan,
Who's a good and great officer.
With the people he's closely linked
As flesh and blood.
Liu Zhidan, O Liu Zhidan,
Who's a good and great officer.

他给人民除痛苦，
他给人民除暴权。
刘志丹，刘志丹，
刘志丹呀是清官，
他给人民以自由，
他给人民分田地。
刘志丹，刘志丹，
刘志丹呀是清官，
他到哪里哪里亮，
他到哪里哪里暖。
跟着刘志丹，
跟着刘志丹，
他让我们享受着永久的幸福，
他让我们的生活更加美满。
跟着刘志丹，
跟着刘志丹，
跟着他，保卫我们的土地，
保卫我们的自由，
保卫苏维埃政权。

He relieves the people's pains,
He eliminates the people's enemies.
Liu Zhidan, O Liu Zhidan,
Who's a good and great officer.
He gives the people freedom they long for,
He gives the people land they strive for.
Liu Zhidan, O Liu Zhidan,
Who's a good and great officer.
He brings light wherever he goes.
He brings warmth wherever he goes.
Let's follow Liu Zhidan,
Ah, let's follow Liu Zhidan,
To enjoy perpetual happiness,
To live a still sweeter life.
Let's follow Liu Zhidan,
Ah, let's follow Liu Zhidan,
To guard our great land,
To guard our precious freedom,
To guard the Soviet power.

（三）

日本鬼子打来啦，
无论穷富一起杀。
鹬蚌相争渔人利，
兄弟们不该再打架。
共产党提出了统一战线，
国共同把日本打。
冬天过去春天到，
豹子川重新又见到春天。
横山，六盘山，
结成了坚固的围；
延水，无定河，
唱着雄壮的歌曲。
这儿是陕甘宁边区，
这儿是民主的抗日根据地。
这儿工人有工作，
这儿农民有田地。
这儿人人说话有权利，
这儿人人都是丰衣足食，
这是自由幸福的新天地，
新呀新天地。

Ⅲ

The Japanese devils are invading our homeland,
A ruffian band kills people rich or poor on the land.
When shepherds quarrel, the wolf has a winning game.
Dear brothers, let's make war on fellow countrymen no more,
Adhere instead to the CPC's unified front tactics,
And get together to fight the Japanese invaders.
After winter comes spring,
And to Baozichuan the springtime does return.
Mount Hengshan, Mount Liupanshan,
Form an unyielding wall;
River Yanshui, River Wuding,
Sing majestic song.
Here is the Shaan-Gan-Ning Border Region,
Here is the Anti-Japanese base area.
Here the workers have jobs,
Here the peasants have land.
Here each and every one enjoys the right of speech,
Here each and every one is well fed and well clad,
Here is the happy land on earth.
A new and happy land on earth.

咱们穿得好，

咱们吃得饱哇，

咱们大家来比赛，

看谁是劳动英雄啊！

劳动英雄真正好，

庄稼种得好呀，下地早啊，

给他戴朵花儿笑一笑。

咱们有自卫军，

咱们有留守兵团，

咱们的意志铁样的强，

咱们的信心钢样的坚。

谁要敢来侵犯我们的美好生活，

就要打死他个王八蛋！

（四）

合水开来了八路军，

一群活泼的青年人，

扛着锄头背着枪，

步伐整齐又精神。

年轻的人年轻的心，

到处是欢笑，

到处是歌声。

Good clothes we wear,
And good food we have,
Now let's race
To be labor heroes!
Glory to these heroes,
For they toil hard and grow good crops,
Let's adorn red flowers on their breasts.
We have self-defense corps;
We have left-behind corps.
Our will is as strong as iron;
Our resolve as firm as steel.
We'll strike dead the bastards
Who dare to disrupt our peaceful life!

Ⅳ

The ERA soldiers are come to Heshui County,
A lively team of young men,
Hoes on shoulder, rifles on back,
Marching in step and in high spirits.
Young men, young hearts,
Everywhere tinkling laughter is heard,
Everywhere joyous songs ring clear and loud.

豹子川从此复活了，
豹子川从此得新生。

你看，什么人一排排工作，
你听，什么人劳动的歌儿高声唱？
尘沙飞起黄土扬，
镐头闪闪放光芒。
你看，他们的劳动多紧张，
你听，他们的歌声多响亮。
挖哟，挖道沟儿起大块哟，
来哟，快来帮个忙啊！
人多手多力气大哟，
大伙一起来下手哇！
小心，小心，当心大块把人伤，
嗨，大块下来了，大块下来了，
这下打进三尺深哪，
小车咕噜咕噜推呀，
推板推土沙沙响啊，
打窑工作忙又忙啊！
今天打进一丈八，
明天打进两丈长。
嗨，咱们来个大突击啊，
自己动手，自己创造，

Oh, Baozichuan, you are born anew,
Oh, Baozichuan, you begin afresh!

Look! Row on row of laborers work hard,
Hark! Song on song ring in the air.
Dust clouds rolling, yellow sand blowing,
Hoes in the sunlight are glowing.
Look! With vigor and valor dwelling caves they are digging,
Hark! Loud and clear they are singing.
O dig, dig, a large clod of clay,
O come, quickly come, lend us helping hands!
More people, more hands, more strength,
Let's work together to get it down!
O beware! Beware! It's too large.
Heigh ho! Down, it's down.
We've dug one meter deep at a single stroke!
Handcarts with clods rumbling on,
Push pedals with earth rustling on,
Digging dwelling caves, hard and busy!
Today we dig six meters deep,
But tomorrow we'll bore much farther.
Hey, a rush job let's do!
We toil and moil with our own hands,

收了果实自己享，

建设也是保边区呀，

前方打仗后方建设都是一样。

大家努力干呀，

努力加油干哪，

车子跑得快哟，

推板走得欢哪，

身上的汗往下淌哟，

休息一会擦把汗哟！

菜儿绿油油，

向我们点点头，

窑洞一排排，

向我们微微笑。

我们的汗流在豹子川哟，

豹子川开了一个大红花。

（主题歌）

党军的骨干，

新中国的青年，

在豹子川扎下大营盘，

把豹子川创建成乐园。

We enjoy the fruits of labor ourselves.
Building up the border region in the rear
Is as fighting the enemy on the front.
On with our work! With redoubled efforts!
With ever-renewed strength and fervour!
Handcarts in flight pass by,
And push pedals flash by.
Drops of sweat trickle down our faces,
Ah, let's take a rest and mop the brows!

Glistening green vegetables
Nod at us;
Row on row of dwelling caves
Smile at us.
We sweat and strain at Baozichuan
Where blooms so splendid a big red flower.

Theme song

The pillar of the Party and the Army,
The youth of New China,
Are stationed at Baozichuan,
Building it into a heavenly paradise on earth.

让豹子川的林更绿，
让豹子川的天更蓝，
让豹子川的荒草变成好地，
让豹子川的荒地变成良田。
把豹子川变成葫芦河，
把豹子川变成南泥湾。
把豹子川变成槐树庄，
把豹子川变成大小凤川！

The forest will be made a most luscious green,
And the sky above even more vast and azure;
Ruins overgrown with weeds will become rich grasslands,
Land, once waste and barren, will be turned into fertile fields.
Learn from Huluhe,
Learn from Nanniwan,
Learn from Huaishuzhuang,
Turn Baozichuan into a rich garner.

陇东中学校歌[①]

在动荡的时代里，
荒漠的原野上，
像孩提的降生，
我们生长，
我们歌唱。
穿过山崖，
穿过海浪，
我们是一群鲜红[②]的孩子，
艰苦团结，
活泼又紧张。
这里是我们生长的地方，
我们要开辟荒凉，

① 这首校歌由时任陇东中学国文兼音乐教师沙垠作词、作曲，约创作于1941年冬或1942年春。

② 据原陇东中学学生王志科回忆录记载，“鲜红”为“天聪”之意。

Song of Longdong Middle School[①]

In the turbulent times,
In the bare wilderness,
Like babes at birth,
We're growing,
And singing.
Over hills and through vales,
And across the wild waves,
We're a group of brilliant children.
Though living a hard life,
We still keep united, alert and lively.
Here is where we were born and raised,
We shall open up the wasteland,

① The music and lyrics of this song were all written by Sha Yin who was then a teacher of Chinese and music at Longdong Middle School in the winter of 1941 or the spring of 1942.

像环江的波涛，

文笔峰的朝阳[1]。

在动荡的时代里，

荒漠的原野上，

我们歌唱，

我们生长。

看金色的黎明，

向我们召唤，

金色的黎明，

向我们召唤。

① 一座与陇东中学隔河相望的山峰。

Like the rolling waves of River Huanjiang,
And the morning glow over Mount Wenbi. ①
In the turbulent times,
In the bare wilderness,
We're singing,
And growing.
Look! The glow of golden dawn
Inspires us to march on forward,
And the glow of golden dawn
Inspires us to march on forward.

① It is a hill which faces Longdong Middle School across the stream.

我们的歌[1]

悠悠的柔水[2]，
滚滚的环江，
人民的子弟欢聚一堂，
勤苦学习，
不分贫富，
积极劳动，
师生一样。
同学们，
我们要学习群众，
服务群众，

① 这首歌曲是由时任陇东中学国文教员程萍作词、国文兼音乐教员苏林作曲，创作于1946年1月。它既是陇东中学的第三首校歌，又是自编的音乐课歌曲之一。

② 柔水，由华池县柔远川流经陇东中学所在地庆城东的河流。它与流经庆城西的环江夹城而过，流汇城南马莲河。

Song of ours[1]

Slow and smooth the Roushui River[2] flows,

Noisy and swift the Huanjiang River goes,

Here, where the youth of our country are happily together.

Study hard,

Be we rich or poor;

Work hard,

Be we teachers or students.

Comrades,

We have to learn from the masses,

Serve the masses,

---

① This song was written in January 1946 with lyrics by Cheng Ping, a teacher of Chinese at Longdong Middle School and music by Su Lin, a teacher of Chinese and music at the same school. It was the third school song of Longdong Middle School and a song taught by the teachers in music class.

② The Roushui River flows from Rouyuanchuan in Huachi County through the east of Qingcheng where Longdong Middle School is located. The Huanjiang River flows through the west of Qingcheng and joins the Roushui River at the south of Qingcheng flowing into the Malian River.

建设陇东做榜样。

亲密团结，

克服困难，

光荣的任务，

我们要承当。

悠悠的柔水，

滚滚的环江，

毛泽东的旗帜下，

新文化放光芒！

And shape Longdong into a model for others.

Closely unite,

Overcome difficulties,

Such sacred duty,

Our shoulders are bearing.

Slow and smooth the Roushui River flows,

Noisy and swift the Huanjiang River goes.

Under the banner of Mao Zedong,

The new culture with radiance glows!

第七章

Chapter Seven

新生活之歌

Songs of New Life

生产小调

（一）

柳叶绿，桃花红，
劳动人民最光荣，
努力生产加油干，
勤苦劳动福满门。

（二）

碗中米，粒粒香，
莫忘汗珠往下淌，
省吃俭用莫浪费，
不怕饥饿和灾荒。

A ditty of production

I

Willow leaves green, peach flowers red,
Most honorable are the laboring people.
To production we put all our strengths
That our life overflows with happiness.

II

Every grain of rice in our bowls smells sweet,
And yet never forget farmers drip with sweat.
Only if we lead our life pinching and scraping,
Are we afraid of hunger and famine no longer.

国庆小唱

太阳一出红又红，
五星红旗飘空中。
新中国成立三年整，
辉煌业绩唱不尽。

土地改革已完成，
全国农民喜盈盈。
有了土地和牛羊，
丰衣足食好光景。

土匪特务都肃清，
社会秩序大安宁。
坚决镇压反革命，
保卫生产莫放松。

抗美援朝齐争光，
捐献的武器数不清。

Song of National Day

The sun comes up red and bright in the sky,
The five-star red flag is flapping on high.
Within three years since it was founded,
New China has made achievements untold.

The Agrarian reforms have been done better,
Joy abides in the hearts of our peasants always.
We're given land and livestock in number greater,
Ample food and clothing assure us of good days.

When bandits and traitors are all eliminated,
Peace and stability brood over the whole nation.
Counter reactionaries are sure to be eradicated,
And to production we must pay enough attention.

To the Korean War everyone puts all his strength,
And the donated weapons we collect are untold.

志愿军个个是英雄，
保家卫国真光荣。

毛主席号召齐响应，
增产节约牢记心。
建设咱们的新中国，
人民江山万年红。

Every volunteer soldier proves brave and bold,
What a glory to keep our country safe and sound!

To Chairman Mao's call all hearts respond well,
Thrift and production increase firmly in our mind dwell.
Let's work as one to build our new China more strong,
So that the people's regime will be forever long.

毛主席是咱的大救星

太阳出来满山红，
毛主席是咱的大救星。

杏花落来桃花开，
毛主席领导咱站起来。

光明大道中间走，
毛主席在咱心里头。

走过了南北又东西，
谁不拥护咱毛主席。

百灵子过河沉不了底，
忘了娘老子忘不了你。

辈辈公鸡辈辈鸣，
跟上咱毛主席闹革命。

Chairman Mao is our big savior

The sun shines on hills red and radiant,
Chairman Mao is our big benefactor.

Peach blossoms blow after apricot flowers fade away,
Chairman Mao leads us towards a still brighter day.

We all walk along the road bright,
In our hearts Chairman Mao sheds his light.

From south to north, from east to west,
All the people love Chairman Mao best.

Larks never drown when they are flying over a river,
Even if we forget our parents we'll remember you forever.

Cocks crow generation after generation,
We follow Chairman Mao for revolution.

人民心向共产党

葵花朵朵向太阳，
人民心向共产党，
葵花向阳结籽稠，
人民靠党幸福长。

The people are true to the Communist Party

As each sunflower turns its face to the sun,
All our hearts go to the Communist Party.
To the sun the sunflower bears seeds many,
With the Party the people live a life happy.

农忙十二月

正月里，正月正，
家家户户迎新春，
积肥送粪整农具，
准备春耕莫放松。

二月里，地开冻，
春暖雪消百草生，
人勤催得春来早，
家家户户忙春耕。

三月里，是清明，
植树造林要抓紧，
房前屋后种瓜豆，
男女老少齐劳动。

四月里，百花香，
青山绿水好风光，

Busy all year long with agricultural work

As the first month by the lunar calendar draws near,
Every family greets spring, beginning of a new year,
Repair farm tools, collect and deliver manure,
To get fully prepared ahead of spring ploughing 'tis sure.

In the second month when spring sings its song,
The ground's thawing, snow melting, grass growing.
It hastens the early spring that people toil all day long,
Every household plunges itself into land furrowing.

In the third month falls the Qingming Festival,
Take the time to plant trees as many as possible;
About the house grow melons, sow beans on the land,
Men and women, young and old, work hand in hand.

In the fourth month myriads of flowers smell sweet,
Green mountains and blue waters, what a wonderful sight!

锄草追肥人人忙，
遍地青苗肥又壮。

五月里，五端阳，
田间管理要加强，
增产措施都落实，
汗水浇来万石粮。

六月里，热难当，
旋黄旋割[①]连声唱，
风摆麦浪金光闪，
龙口夺食抢收忙。

七月里，三伏天，
抓紧伏耕莫怠慢，
秋田作物勤管理，
抢墒复种夺丰产，

八月里，瓜果香，
糜子谷子齐上场，
细打扬净快入仓，

① 旋黄旋割，布谷鸟，每年小麦成熟收割期间天天鸣叫，似乎在催农夫快割抢收。

Weeding and fertilizing farm fields, no idle hand around,
Young crops, fat and firm, growing all over the ground.

The fifth month sees the Dragon Boat Festival,
To grow good crops a wise management of field we make,
To increase production effective measures we take,
And to reap a bumper harvest countless drops of sweat we shed.

The sixth is so hot a month we're hard to spend,
Cuckoo birds are cooing as one voice on end.
Wheat fields waving in the wind glitter like gold,
Farmers busy reaping when the weather is good.

With lunar July comes the hottest month of the year,
Take time by the forelock, and plough the cropland;
Sow seeds when there's enough moisture in the land,
And take care of crops in autumn fields which stand.

In the eighth month fruits waft sweet smell around,
The harvest is gathered on the threshing ground.
Hurry to do the threshing, winnowing and storing,

丰收早缴爱国粮。

九月里，天渐冷，
农时节令不等人，
冬麦播种要赶紧，
来年才有好收成。

十月里，天气寒，
粮食入仓农事闲，
男修水利女深翻，
年年莫忘整农田。

十一月，雪花飘，
千车万担积肥料，
喂好牲口勤垫圈，
副业生产人人搞。

十二月，一年整，
生产计划要早订，
编耱[①]打筐修农具，
趁早着手迎新春。

---

① 耱，平整土地的一种农具。

And never forget to deliver tax grain to the state.

In the ninth month the weather turns chill,
For no man the farming seasons wait will,
Use our time to plant winter wheat soonest,
And next year we'll reap a bumper harvest.

When the tenth month advances, the air grows wintry,
Farming work's done, grain's in garners of the country.
Men begin irrigation work, women turn up the soil here,
Remember well that fields need to be leveled every year.

In the eleventh month snowflakes fall from the sky,
Feed livestock well and spread earth in stall and pigsty,
Collect thousand cartloads or basketfuls of manure we may;
To link sideline to production everybody's happy and gay.

The twelfth month means a year comes to the end,
Be sure to make production plans ahead for next year.
Weave new Moes① and baskets, farm tools mend,
Ready to hail a happy new year when it draws near.

---

① Mo, a kind of farm tools used to level the soil.

献上颂歌献上心

（合）太阳出来一点红，
万水千山一个音。
陇东儿女想恩人，
唱一曲山歌表深情。

（男）天上星星哪一颗亮？
地下江河哪一条长？
什么人恩情大无比，
领导人民得解放？

（女）天上星星北斗亮，
地下河流长江长，
毛主席恩情大无比，
领导人民得解放。

（男）什么树木四季青？
什么花开花最红？

Singing songs with our hearts

(C) The sun rises from the east like a red spot,
Ten thousand hearts sing to the same chord.
Longdong people miss our savior so much,
We sing our love and thanks to him in chorus.

(M) Which star up in the sky shines the brightest?
Which river down on the earth is the longest?
Whose kindness to us is the greatest?
Who steers the people to liberation?

(F) Up in the sky the Big Dipper shines the brightest,
Down on the earth the Changjiang River is the longest;
Chairman Mao's kindness to us is the greatest,
And it is he who steers the people to liberation.

(M) What tree stays evergreen all year round?
What flower comes in blossom bright red?

什么人活在咱心里，
千秋万代留英名？

（女）山上松柏四季青，
石榴花开花最红，
周总理活在咱心里，
千秋万代留英名。

（男）什么坚来什么硬？
什么展翅闯风云？
什么人带领百万兵，
南征北战创奇功？

（女）磐石坚来钢铁硬，
雄鹰展翅闯风云，
朱老总带领百万兵，
南征北战创奇功。

（合）一句歌儿一片情，
献上颂歌献上心，
陇东儿女跟党走，
千秋万代向前进。

Who dwells deep in our hearts forevermore?
Whose fame continues to grow forevermore?

(F) Pines and cypresses stay evergreen all year round,
Blossoms on pomegranate trees bloom bright red;
Premier Zhou dwells deep in our hearts forevermore,
And his fame continues to grow also forevermore.

(M) What is the hardest and strongest thing under the sun?
What bird cleaves the clouds into the dark skies?
Who has taken tens of thousands of soldiers
And on many fronts worked heroic wonders?

(F) Nothing under the sun is hard as rock, strong as steel,
The eagle spreads its wings to soar through the clouds;
Commander-in-chief Zhu led millions of soldiers,
Fought north and south, and worked heroic wonders.

(C) A sweet song expresses a deep feeling,
To offer our loyal hearts we are singing.
The Longdong people follow the Party,
And march on forward from year to year.

五哥放羊唱新曲

春季里来百草长，
满山牛羊闹嚷嚷，
富民政策指富路，
五哥放羊心欢畅。

夏季里来麦穗黄，
五哥放羊高山唱，
欢歌迎来四方客，
致富花开满院香。

秋季里来秋风凉，
妹缝新衣郎换上，
五哥放羊唱新曲，
商品经济前程广。

冬季里来腊梅香，
五哥放羊美名扬，
专业户里数第一，
五哥登上光荣榜。

Wu Ge a shepherd boy sings a new song

When spring comes, a hundred grasses sprout,
Over the mountain cows and goats roam about.
The Party's good policy shows us a golden way,
While keeping sheep Wu Ge feels happy and gay.

When summer is near, golden are the grain ears,
Herding his sheep on the hill Wu Ge gaily sings.
His songs of joy are heard by guests from afar,
Praise for a happier life the people live by far.

When autumn approaches, the wind blows cold,
Wu Ge changes into the new clothes I've sewed.
His songs tell a different story from the days old,
Singing praises of the commercial economy good.

Winter comes laden with mume blossoms sweet,
Far and near my Wu Ge becomes renowned.
He stands first among specialized household,
And his name appearing on the honor board.

新唱《绣金匾》

五月里五端阳，
金匾绣得忙，
七彩线巧搭配，
心中话儿都绣上。

一绣陕甘宁，
南梁红旗展，
为革命立功勋，
西北红了天。

二绣红太阳，
照得东方亮，
建立了新中国，
人民翻身得解放。

三绣百花香，
改革开放好主张，

A new version of *Embroidering the Golden Banner*

On the Dragon Boat Festival in May lunar,
We're busy embroidering the golden banner,
On it are words from the depth of our hearts,
Stitched skillfully with more colorful threads.

We embroider the Shaan-Gan-Ning Border Region,
High above Nanliang the red flags are streaming,
Against the skies above Northwest China flaming,
Great contributions it's made to the Chinese revolution.

We embroider the red sun,
Whose light brightens the east.
When New China was founded,
The people have been liberated.

We embroider myriads of fragrant flowers,
The reform and opening up proves a good policy,

春天的故事荡春雷，
祖国山河大变样。

四绣金凤凰，
百鸟齐飞翔，
“三个代表”指方向，
和谐社会多吉祥。

五绣谷穗长，
种地不纳粮，
科学发展百业旺呀，
老百姓喜洋洋。

六绣南梁人，
齐心求真理，
铸就千秋不朽业呀，
我们永传承。

Like the thunder of spring over our land rumbling,
Arousing the hills and rivers in heavy slumbering.

We embroider phoenixes, fair and golden,
Who fly high along with flocks of birds.
"Three Represents" show us the way onwards,
Making our land harmonious and auspicious.

We embroider ears of grain, fat and long,
All farmers pay the grain tax no longer;
All business based on science is fast growing,
All people wear faces with happiness glowing.

We embroider Nanliang people, pure and kind,
Who seek the truth with one heart and mind,
And make monumental achievements untold,
Which we are sure to keep and hand onward.

参考文献

白学锋，罗凯，2010．陇东老区革命歌谣发展的历程述略［J］．社科纵横（12）：89－92．

丁祖馨，2001．中国诗歌集（英汉对照）［M］．沈阳：辽宁大学出版社．

段方，等，2002．浪漫英语诗歌（英汉对照）［M］．合肥：安徽科学技术出版社．

高文，巩世锋，2011．陇东红色歌谣［M］．兰州：甘肃人民出版社．

巩世锋，2015．陇东：说不完的革命故事［M］．兰州：甘肃文化出版社．

顾桐山，2008．中国民间情歌精选［M］．哈尔滨：黑龙江美术出版社．

郭含殿，2007．华池歌谣［M］．兰州：甘肃人民出版社．

何功杰，2002．英美名诗品读［M］．上海：上海交通大学出版社．

何天明，1986．汉英英汉对照歌曲 100 首［M］．南昌：江西人民出版社.

胡家峦，1995. 英语诗歌精品（英汉对照）[M]. 北京：北京大学出版社.

南开大学外文系，1959. 中国新民歌选（汉英对照，上下册）[M]. 北京：商务印书馆.

帕尔格雷夫，1987. 英诗金库（英汉对照，上下卷）[M]. 罗义蕴，曹明伦，陈朴，编注. 成都：四川人民出版社.

秦希廉，1992. 英语短诗精选（英汉对照）[M]. 北京：知识出版社.

秦秀白，等，2000. 七彩的梦 英语精彩歌谣欣赏（英汉对照）[M]. 武汉：华中理工大学出版社.

人民教育出版社外语室英语组，1989. 英语诗歌集［M］. 北京：人民教育出版社.

尚怀晓，1973. 革命歌曲选（汉英对照，上下册）[M]. 上海：上海人民出版社.

汪国真，2013. 诗情于此终结：汉英对照汪国真诗选[M]. 蒋隆国，译. 北京：清华大学出版社.

王贵禄，2015. 陇东红色歌谣：政治美学、革命记忆及民间叙事［J］. 文艺理论与批评（3）：136 - 143.

王宏印，2009. 西北回响——汉英对照新旧陕北民歌[M]. 北京：文化艺术出版社.

吴松林，2012. 江格尔（汉英对照，上下册）[M]. 长春：吉林大学出版社.

肖鹏，2003．中学生英语诗歌精选[M]．广州：广东世界图书出版公司.

熊若磐，梁联发，2003．汉英对照怀旧金曲［M］．上海：上海音乐出版社.

许渊冲，1984．翻译的艺术（论文集）[C]．北京：中国对外翻译出版公司.

许渊冲，2000．汉英对照唐诗三百首[M]．北京：高等教育出版社.

许渊冲，2009．元明清诗（汉英对照）[M]．北京：中国对外翻译出版公司.

许渊冲，2014．许渊冲英译白居易诗选（汉英对照）[M]．北京：中国对外翻译出版有限公司.

许渊冲，2014．许渊冲英译杜甫诗选（汉英对照）[M]．北京：中国对外翻译出版有限公司.

许渊冲，2014．许渊冲英译李白诗选（汉英对照）[M]．北京：中国对外翻译出版有限公司.

许渊冲，2014．许渊冲英译王维诗选（汉英对照）[M]．北京：中国对外翻译出版有限公司.

许渊冲，2015．许渊冲英译毛泽东诗词（汉英对照）[M]．北京：中译出版社.

颜健生，2014．瑶族民歌选译（汉英对照）[M]．武汉：华中科技大学出版社.
张文诺，2012. 论陇东红色歌谣的主题诉求［J］. 井冈山大学学报：社会科学版（6）：19－25.
张文诺，2014. 论陇东红色歌谣的文化学阐释［J］. 井冈山大学学报：社会科学版（4）：21－27.
赵晓阳，2006. 旧京歌谣［M］. 北京：北京图书馆出版社.
中国文学出版社，1998. 中国文学：古代诗歌卷［M］. 北京：外语教学与研究出版社.
中国文学出版社，1998. 中国文学：现代诗歌卷［M］. 北京：外语教学与研究出版社.
A'RABBITT S，2009. China rhymes：two classics of coast China poetry［M］. Hong Kong：Earnshaw Books.

后 记

写诗不易，译诗更难，汉语诗歌译成英语更是难上加难。民谣虽不是诗歌，不如诗词那么晦涩，也没有诗词严格的韵律，但是民谣翻译作为诗歌翻译的特殊类型，在忠实原文内容的基础上，也要重视节奏感、音韵美与形式美的再现，尽量保留原歌谣的语言、情感、意象、意境和风格，注重译文流畅达意和诗味传达，强调整体翻译效果。就此而言，民谣的翻译难度并不亚于诗歌。在翻译陇东红色歌谣的过程中，我深切体验到翻译之难与翻译者的不易。译者不能像作者一样自由、潇洒地创作，从而得到抒发的满足；翻译的工作就像是被绑着手脚“耍杂技”，还要耍得有水平，达到翻译作品的“信、达、雅”或者“意美、音美、形美”三美齐备的境界，的确不易。

《陇东红色歌谣选译》经过专家评审被列为2018年庆阳市重点文艺创作资助项目。在出版之际，又得到了陇东学院学术著作出版基金的资助。更幸运的是，我于同年获得前往北京语言大学访学一年的宝贵机会，为翻译工作赢得了时间和资源。本书的修改完善工作是我访学期间在导师王雅华教授指导下完成的。

两年来，我将全部闲暇时间都用于读书与翻译，尤其在访学的一年里，更是全身心投入。日复一日，寒来暑往，其中的艰辛不堪回首。自知学养不足，因此更需苦心孤诣，一丝不苟。在翻译过程中，我仔细阅读了英美诗歌和汉语诗歌、歌谣英译书籍六十余册，反复推敲韵律，锤炼词句，斟酌结构，逐步完善，正如清代诗人袁牧《遣兴》诗云：“爱好由来下笔难，一诗千改始心安。”漫游书海，获益匪浅，他山之石，为我所用，本书在翻译细节上不仅仿效英美诗人，还吸收了前人译笔精华。最令我难以忘怀的翻译前辈当属“书销中外百余本，诗译英法唯一人”的中国著名古诗词翻译家许渊冲教授，他翻译的诗词使我爱不忍释、百读不厌。许渊冲注重“意美、音美和形美”，他将中国诗词译出了韵和境，使中国的古诗词在翻译成外文时带上了特有的中国味儿——那种长袖而歌的汉韵，同时也将美感发挥到了极致，从而使它们走向了世界，他的巨大贡献令世人望尘莫及。目前，民歌英译研究方兴未艾，有许多相关论文和译著出版。谨以此书抛砖引玉，期望引起更多人对陇东民歌英译的关注，从而使陇东民歌真正地走出国门，走向世界。

成书付梓之际，感谢《陇东红色歌谣》原编者高文和巩世锋两位先生在搜集、整理、选编陇东红色歌谣过程中付出的辛勤劳动；感谢76岁高龄的伯父，陇东学院原中文系主任，校党委宣传部部长闫果知教授，没有他的提议、策划、解读与鼓励，无以成此书；感谢我的访学导师王雅华教授的悉心指导；感谢外籍教师 Keenan Madson 审阅译稿；感谢陇东学院外国语学院李旭教授百忙之中审定译稿并提出宝贵的修改意见；感谢远在澳大利亚的同窗好友白琳女士倾情相助；感谢家人的理解、支持与帮扶，使我更加执着于自己的追求；也愿此书与读研的儿子共勉，在求学的道路上我们不懈努力，砥砺前行。

歌谣翻译工作难度很大，既要坚持“信”和“达”的要求，又要尽量保持原文的“雅”与神韵；既要讲究意美，又要兼具音美与形美，极富挑战性。由于译者学养不足，能力有限，时间紧迫，译文疏漏在所难免，恳请专家学者批评指正。

闫晓茹

2019 年 10 月于陇东学院